*What*

The Life

"As a man, I've never understood why women had to lug their handbags around, until I read this book—now I know!"

**– Tyler R. Tichelaar, Ph.D. and Award-Winning Author of *The Best Place***

"A unique look into the world of a woman's life and the relationship with her handbags. A fun thoughtful girlie romp, even men will laugh."

**– Patrick Snow, International Best Selling Author of *Creating Your Own Destiny* and *The Affluent Entrepreneur***

"I have to wonder, after reading this book, what goes on in my closet when I'm not looking! I hope my bags are having a wonderful time! Thanks for this fun book!"

**– Micki McWade, Author of *Getting Up, Getting Over, Getting On: a Twelve Step Guide to Divorce Recovery* and *Daily Meditations for Surviving a Breakup, Separation or Divorce*, Speaker, Coach and handbag lover**

"Once you read this fun, creative and innovative book, you'll never look at a handbag the same way again."

— **Susan Friedmann, CSP, International Best-Selling Author of** *Riches in Niches: How to Make it BIG in a small Market*

"Only a creative genius can come up with this concept. It will make you look at everything in your closet differently."

— **Michael Fulmore, Author of** *Releasing Your Ambition*

"I always felt my handbags had a life of their own. This book confirms it. I highly recommend this entertaining, unique book."

— **Andrea Donsky, Author of** *Unjunk Your Junk Food* **& Founder of NaturallySavvy.com**

"This book is a charmer! I never expected to enjoy the story of a handbag that talks so much, but it's really wonderful. The conversations with other handbags, the way they all feel about their owner, "She"... It was a total delight, winning me over more and more with each chapter. The character "She" is complex and very real, and subtly draws you in as she moves through the ups and downs of a modern woman's life. A great, fun read, and a story that I hope continues. (And it will make a perfect gift for my wife!)"

— **Andy Weisberg, Author of** *Laid Off & Crazy Happy – The Memoirs of a Houseband*

"Gentlemen wouldn't it be fun to understand the underlying behaviors most women exhibit? Here is your chance. In The Life & Times of Lorna Rae one finds a wonderful and easy read that sheds light on most women and their behaviors. I fully recommend this funny and witty book."

**– Dana Arias, Author of *Dear Parents, From Your Child's Loving Teacher***

"Toy Story had me giddy thinking that my toys could be alive, watching and helping me in ways I didn't know. Now, due to Lorna Faxon, I see my handbags in a new light. The Life & Times of Lorna Rae is a fabulous read and gives you a very new perspective on life."

**– Siobhan A. Stevens, Author of *Bleeding Indy***

# The Life & Times of

*Lorna Rae*

A Novel

# L. Faxon

**The Life & Times of Lorna Rae:** *A Novel*
Copyright ©2013 Lorna Faxon

This book is a work of fiction. Names, characters, businesses, organizations, places, events, and incidents either are the product of the author's imagination or are used fictitiously. Any resemblance to actual persons, living or dead, events, or locales is entirely coincidental.

Address all inquiries to:
Lorna Faxon
www.LornaRae.com

Published by:
Aviva Publishing
Lake Placid, NY
518-523-1320
www.avivapubs.com

Editor: Tyler Tichelaar
Cover & Interior Design: Fusion Creative Works

Hardcover: 978-1-940984-38-4
Paperback: 978-1-940984-74-2
eBook: 978-1-938686-80-1
Library of Congress Control Number: 2013915770

Second Printing
Printed in the United States of America

For additional copies please visit: www.LornaRae.com

# Dedication

*To my best girlfriends and my favorite handbags;*
*you know who you are.*

# Contents

# Chapter One
# H = HELP

*Barbra Streisand: "Is love so blind?"*
*Yves Montand: "No, it's that mistrust*
*is so exhausting..."*
*— On A Clear Day You Can See Forever*

## | SHE |

She entered the stairwell, clasping her Lorna Rae handbag against her chest like it was a precious child. What had just happened to her life? Where did she go from here? She released the bag to her arm so she could navigate the stairs. The tears stung her eyes as she fought them back, causing them to swim in her sockets, unable to be released and fall. She ran down each flight and clutched the handrail to avoid any kind of tumble. She was already in enough emotional pain that the thought of any physical injury was unacceptable. A few tears escaped from her eyes and landed on her handbag.

When She reached the bottom, she pushed the door open and felt the sun hit her face and dry out the tears. Freedom was closing in. The bag slid down her arm and was warmly clasped in her hand. She slowed her gait so she wouldn't draw attention to her current emotional state and headed for the street to find a cab; however, She kept walking in no particular direction. She needed to decide her next move—where to go. For now, she could disappear in the crowd along the city sidewalk. Even though she had walked this path a thousand times, she didn't see anything familiar.

She took in several deep breaths to calm down, but she stopped herself, realizing she needed to feel this moment, not take it away from herself. Did she really just quit her job? Leaving with only her lovely handbag on her arm? Did she have to go back to collect her books, photos, artwork, and awards? Could she send a friend to collect those items? There was no way her pride would let her return. They didn't deserve to see her again. The betrayal weighed on her heart and made her feel ill.

After several blocks of feeling numb, She looked up and saw the French bakery ahead and decided that would be her next move. Pastry and coffee were her comfort foods. She had learned earlier to be kind to herself in a crisis. Some would view this as selfish, but She knew it was survival. She entered the bakery and was immediately comforted by the smell of freshly baked cakes. She slowly gazed at the pastry display case and decided on chocolate cake and a shot of espresso. Tough times call for C&C (chocolate and caffeine). She approached the counter after scanning the case. "I'll take the chocolate cake and a shot of espresso," she said. The waitress asked whether it was for here or to go. She replied, "For here, please." She retrieved the wallet from her handbag and paid in cash.

"How is your afternoon going?" the perky waitress asked. "Fine," She responded. She hoped the tears were gone from her eyes, but she was worried the emotion was on her face or in her bloodshot eyes. She had not had a chance to check her face with the small hand mirror in the pocket of her purse. The little flip mirror had been given to her by a close friend who brought it back from Paris. It had a lovely picture of the Eiffel Tower. Ah, Paris, another comfort.

The waitress handed her the gorgeous cake on a plate and the shot in the tiny cup with saucer. She loved to order coffee this way. It made her feel like she was at a small child's tea party.

She made her way toward a table and was trying to decide whether she wanted to sit along the front and watch people or hide in the back. She decided to sit in front and watch the people go by—a nice distraction. She placed the Lorna Rae handbag on the chair next to her and took a sip of her espresso. The hot mixture felt delicious and bitter at the same time; She felt her stomach flip and didn't feel like eating the cake. The events of the day washed over her.

She watched as people passed by, and she wondered who they were and how they lived, whether they were happy, married, single, wealthy, struggling, employed. It was something she did sometimes when she traveled and drove through neighborhoods—passing houses and wondering who lived there and what their lives were like; what would it be like to be them? Why did she have the life she did?

She noticed an elderly woman at the next table watching her, and they exchanged a small smile. The Woman made a gentle hand gesture toward her selection and stated, "You must be celebrating or having a bad day."

She smiled, but at the same time, the interaction stirred something in her and the tears sprang up and ran down her cheeks.

The Woman immediately got up and moved to her table, touching her shoulder, "There, there, dear; it can't be that bad."

She was horrified and comforted at the same time; She rarely cried and never in public.

The Woman handed her a tissue from her vintage but chic handbag. It was a crocodile brown clutch from the '40s. The Woman set the clutch on the table near the chair by the Lorna Rae and sat in the remaining vacant chair.

"Now tell me all about it when you are ready," said the Woman, and She had to stifle the cry that was wanting to scream its escape from her body.

She didn't answer right away because she was trying to figure out what to say. Should she go into detail or just give the *Reader's Digest* version? She didn't know this woman, and after what she had been through, she wasn't exactly in the mood to trust anyone. But looking into the Woman's kind face, She decided to take a chance and tell just the highlights of the events that had taken place. The Woman listened and nodded and then reached across the table and patted her hand.

"I can tell you are a good person, and some day when the pain has passed, you are going to be better than before. Trust this old lady; I have seen it all, and when you let things go, they will come to you. But for now, you need to enjoy your cake and finish your coffee. I want to invite you to dinner, and I won't take no for an answer."

She noticed the Woman's vintage handbag and commented on its beauty. "Such a lovely clutch; where did you find such an incredible piece?"

"My husband brought it back for me on his way back through the Panama Canal after World War II. I know it's a little outdated, but it's sentimental, so I use it once in awhile to lift my spirits."

"It doesn't look outdated, and even though it's vintage, the texture and cut are exquisite."

"Thank you, dear; someday I will show you my collection; I have a weakness for handbags."

"Me too. I don't have that many, but those I do have are so special to me."

"A good handbag is such an important part of a woman's personality and life."

"Indeed," She replied.

They both smiled and took a sip of their coffee to contemplate their appreciation for their handbags; they gazed at theirs with admiration and to make sure they were in a safe place. A woman should always be aware of the location of her handbag.

She couldn't believe how easy it was to talk to her new friend, and before she knew it, she had finished her coffee and most of the chocolate cake. They exchanged phone numbers and pleasantries as they said goodbye for now.

She suddenly felt like a small lifeline had been extended and her outlook was about to change.

## | LORNA RAE |

Lorna Rae knew something was up when She raised her voice; its stern and motherly tone could be referenced, but this was something new, and it grabbed Lorna Rae's attention. The handbag had been with She for several years, which in a handbag's life would be long-term.

The management job She held was over; the words had been spoken and it was time to leave. Lorna Rae had never been prouder. She had suffered for months, and the betrayal of those She had given so much to was more than she could bear. She had tried to navigate and repair the damage, but enough was enough. Lorna Rae would later hear She reference one of these outrageous comments against her with a sense of humor. "If people were that afraid of me and I had that much power, I should be running a small country somewhere." But they weren't afraid of her; they were jealous, insecure, and frightened of their own job mortality. But to her detriment, She had failed to play the game and had let down her guard.

Lorna Rae could still hear She's final words, the strength of her convictions, and the support of her mentors. The universe would handle those left behind.

Even in her state, She had remembered to remove her company badge and office door key from the handbag and place it on her desk before leaving the office. She strode out with her head held high and passed the elevator to avoid any further human contact. She entered the stairwell and clutched Lorna Rae to her chest as if to hug a friend in need. Lorna Rae was then moved to hang from She's arm as she headed down the stairs. Jostling on She's arm, the handbag felt the emotion of the situation; a few teardrops hit the side of her fabric and startled Lorna Rae. Once they reached the street, Lorna Rae was shifted to She's hand and she felt She squeeze the handle.

When they entered the bakery, Lorna Rae could smell the buttery croissants and fresh coffee. Knowing She needed some C&C, Lorna Rae was hoping they wouldn't stay too long so the smells of the shop didn't penetrate her lambskin cover.

However, given She's condition, Lorna Rae was happy to be there and hoping another interesting handbag would be near for a conversation.

Lorna Rae noticed the other handbag resting on the café table. The vintage brown crocodile exterior was worn. Lorna Rae was reluctant to start up a conversation, and a lot like her owner, she was usually shy to initiate any interaction when confronted with a stranger. It humored her to notice how handbags were sometimes a reflection of their owners—a lot like dogs. This one was well-loved, older, and it held a lifetime of experiences. She looked back and forth between the owner and the handbag and decided to let today go by without a conversation. Also, the bag seemed to be happy napping. The flap of the bag was open and Lorna Rae could see inside it; she noticed the bulging wallet that looked uncomfortable, stuffed with several credit cards and receipts; the hairbrush was thick with strands and had not been cleaned out since the Reagan administration. Lorna Rae imagined the bottom of the bag was littered with Kleenex, loose cough drops, coins, and bobby pins.

## | SHE |

After her visit at the bakery, She went straight home. She would normally set down Lorna Rae on the hallway table, but she went straight to the master bedroom walk-in closet. It was her favorite room in the apartment, her sanctuary, where designer garments and handbags were hung with care, and the shelves were lined with precious handbags, shoes, and token fashion memorabilia, which included various shopping bags, Chanel and Tiffany boxes, Lanvin jewelry boxes, and some of her Hollywood vintage movie star collectibles such as an Elizabeth Taylor pillbox and a tiny tray that once belonged to Rita Hayworth.

She set Lorna Rae on the bench and immediately shed off her clothes and departed for the bathroom to fill the tub. There was nothing like a good lavender bubble bath to calm her nerves and reduce stress. She sank into the bubbles, letting out a sigh of relief, and a flood of tears were to follow. A good cry was in order. It wasn't the fear of survival because She had a significant nest egg; it was the emotional betrayal and damage to her self-esteem that hurt most of all. Because after all, one's reputation is significant, and such an attack can evoke a primal reaction.

After the bath, all She wanted to do was put on a nightgown and go to bed. Tonight was the one night she was so tired that a sleep aid would not be necessary. Instead, She got dressed for her dinner engagement and put on a pair of Jil Sander slacks, Akris top, Prada coat, and Manolo Blahnik shoes, and after scanning the shelf of handbags, she decided there wasn't enough time to make the change and decided to carry Lorna Rae for the evening. She was due at the Woman's house and was curious and interested to see what the evening had in store.

### | LORNA RAE |

Lorna Rae wasn't sure what was in order when they arrived home and headed straight to the closet. This move probably meant the handbag would be staying home tonight and one of the smaller bags would be going out for the evening. After that day's events, that was fine with her, although she was curious about visiting the new friend. After Lorna Rae was placed on the bench and She departed for the tub, Lorna Rae let out a sigh and looked up at the shelf to see her roommates looking down with great curiosity. They sensed something was up due to She being home sooner than normal, her body language, and the late afternoon bath.

*Lorna Rae is a classic double handle style handbag available in various colors of lambskin with a beautiful fob hanging from one of the sturdy handles. This particular Lorna Rae is black and the fob is sold separately so each owner can purchase the one of her choice. This Lorna Rae has a fob made of crystals, rhinestones, and pearls. It has a top zipper enclosure and practical lining with the LR monogram embroidered in red on the interior. This is the elegant subtle sign that indicates the bags label.*

Once the coast was clear, it was the Prada Limited Edition Paisley Pattern tote style bag that spoke first.

"What happened?"

"She quit her job today," said Lorna Rae.

They all gasped and started to talk at once. "What will we do? You know what could happen?" They were not strangers to being transferred to another owner via the consignment shop. She had acquired most of the designer bags there. YSL Easy was not aware of this procedure since she was purchased at Neiman Marcus and was frightened by the possibility of leaving the comfort of the closet and the owner she adored.

*An instant hit when it was launched in 2008, the YSL Easy handbag came hot on the heels of the Muse, which had already become an accessory sensation the world over. Bigger, bolder, and with a little more of a laid back, rock-chic vibe, the Easy was in the right place at the right time for instant "It Bag" status. Early versions made from pebbled leather were a particularly huge hit.*

Who would be the first to go? Would it be those She tended to take out the least? Would it be those who held the most resale value? Would it be the beautiful beaded Fendi Baguette, the Prada LE Paisley, the YSL Metallic Easy Bag, the Lanvin Pop Leather Clutch, the Balenciaga City bag, the Louis Vuitton Cherry Pochette, the Green Longchamp Roseau Croco, the Chanel Paris Biarritz handbag tote, the Dolce & Gabbana "Miss Lexington" black lambskin bag, or finally, the beaded evening bag that once belonged to movie star, Natalie Wood?

Lorna Rae encouraged the handbags to calm down and not to panic, but the handbags were quick to point out that Lorna Rae, being the favorite and coveted bag, would be the last to go. Lorna Rae also tried to remind them that She typically changed out and sold her clothing more than the handbags.

They could hear She approaching, and they were a bit surprised when She didn't change out to a smaller bag and took Lorna Rae with her. Their suspicions were confirmed; Lorna Rae was the favorite. However, the real reason was that She was too tired to change to a smaller bag, and She didn't want to be late for her dinner appointment.

Once She and Lorna Rae left, the other bags broke into conversation all at once and their paranoia took over as they speculated on what would happen next.

"Do you really think she will get rid of some of us now that she is not working?" they kept asking.

The Prada, who was the newest member of the closet, was quiet. The others continued their conversation.

"You know she will get rid of the one she uses the least." And they looked in the direction of the Balenciaga, who responded with defensiveness. "Even though I don't leave the closet as much, I know she would not get rid of me first…I would think the Dolce & Gabbana would go first."

Although the Balenciaga did not feel reassured, her resale value was high, and she was not the first Balenciaga to leave the closet from what she knew from the other bags.

They all were talking at once…. The smaller handbags also felt threatened because they knew they did not go out as often as the others. The Fendi and Louis Vuitton glanced at each other and did not say a word. Finally, the Prada spoke up and convinced the group to calm down and not jump to any conclusions until they could find out more when Lorna Rae returned. Some of the others were not so convinced, but they realized that stressing any more was not a good idea.

*Mario Prada started the Prada label in 1913. He designed and sold trunks, suitcases, shoes, and handbags through two boutiques in Milan and had clients across Europe and the United States. In 1978, Mario's granddaughter, Miuccia Prada, took over the company and evolved it into a major powerhouse in luxury fashion design. The Prada LE Paisley bag is a simple medium size sturdy tote with two black hinged handles in the front, a black piping accent, and a fun paisley exterior design.*

The vintage evening bag was not too afraid of being removed from the closet due to her unique history, and she was necessary for formal functions. The less exp-sive Longchamp was not as worried either since her resa value was not enough to be sent away, but still, there were times when bags like her would leave on one of She's closet clean-outs.

## | SHE |

She found a cab as soon as she left her apartment. She gave the driver the address for her new friend's building. When She arrived, it was apparent her new friend had means and was probably not a threat to her safety. It was not like She to trust someone so quickly, but her instincts told her this was someone she wanted to get to know.

After the doorman let her in, She headed to the elevator. As she walked through the elegant lobby, she caught her reflection in the large mirror and could see she needed to run a comb through her hair again. The minute She was on the elevator and the door closed, she pulled out a small brush from her bag to straighten out her unkempt locks. Even though she had tried to take care in looking presentable, it was obvious the day had taken its toll.

When the elevator reached the Woman's floor, She stepped off and found the correct apartment; then she rang the bell. She was greeted by a distinguished gentleman in a tuxedo, and as she crossed the threshold, She felt she was stepping into a Cary Grant movie.

"Good evening," said the gentleman. "I am Charles. May I take your coat?" She shed the Black Prada coat and handed it to him along with her handbag.

"Thank you," She said as he hung it up.

"Madam is waiting in the living room," said Charles. "Please follow me."

They walked through the marble entry, passing a round entry table with an enormous bouquet of fresh flowers in a stunning vase. She could hear her Manola Blahnik heels on the marble floor as they approached the living room, and the light tapping ended when She entered the carpeted living room. The softness of the floor below her feet felt like a cushion of clouds and She relaxed even more.

"Ah, there you are!" She's new friend exclaimed. "I am so glad you came, and you look lovely. Now, first things first, a cocktail is in order. What may we get you, my dear?"

"I would love a martini."

"Excellent choice. Make it two, Charles."

"Yes, Madam," Charles replied and departed as She approached her new friend with a warm hug.

"Now, my dear," said the Woman, "come in and s. down and let's talk and discuss nothing in particular but talk about everything. Let me be a distraction for you this evening since you had enough emotion for the day, and you can face all those decisions tomorrow. Let's get to know each other, and since I'm an old lady who's not afraid of much of anything these days, you will discover that I am not afraid to take over a conversation; therefore, I will go first."

She adored her candid and entertaining new friend. She felt like she had entered the realm of a modern day Auntie Mame.

At one point in the evening, after dinner and before they had dessert and coffee in the living room, they went on a tour of the amazing penthouse. Everything was comfortable and elegant, but the master bedroom closet was the room that made She's jaw drop. When the light went on, She looked up and saw the chandelier that made the room sparkle. The clothes were lined up and arranged by color and height, but the thing that caught her attention was the area that held all the handbags. Some were enclosed in lighted cases that looked like they were on display in a museum. She gravitated toward the cases and peered in at the collection of vintage and current Chanel handbags. They took her breath away.

"Is that a vintage Chanel 2.55 along with the current version?" She asked.

"Oh yes, one of my favorites," said the Woman.

"I can see that, and I agree," said She. "It's on my list to have someday."

Her new friend smiled and told her to open the case and take a look at it.

"Are you sure?" She asked. "This is too good; these are amazing." She felt like a kid in a candy store, but instead of candy, the collection of rare and beautiful handbags were She's drug of choice.

They spent a good hour in the closet going through the history of each bag and where She's friend got it and where she went with some of them and what they meant to her. She's favorite was a bright pink patent leather Lady Dior that seemed just to glow.

"Oh, may I take it out?" She asked.

"Of course. This bag is also one of my favorites, but I'm afraid I just don't use it as much as I should. In fact, most of these lovely handbags just hang out here looking good but have nowhere to go."

There were a few Hermes Birken bags and a fur Fendi, a small case of Judith Leiber evening bags, and whimsical Lulu Guinness bags. There were Gucci, Louis Vuitton,

Mulberry, YSL, Jimmy Choo, and a few Fendi baguett bags. Another case held some vintage alligator and crocodile bags by Robert Capucci and a few Lucite handbags from the 1950s. It was hard to leave this little bit of paradise, but it was getting late, and the smell of the fresh coffee made them retreat back to the living room to enjoy the ritual and finish the evening.

She could hardly believe it was 11:30 p.m. when the conversation took a lull and She stifled a yawn.

The Woman said, "Well, this has been a lovely evening, and we must do it again soon. In fact, I am going to my country estate in two weeks, and I think the fresh air and quiet would do you some good."

It sounded lovely, and She was quick to accept the invitation. They said their goodnights, and then her new friend left her with a nugget of wisdom, "Don't forget we find great beauty and learning in our trials."

Before She could request a cab, Charles informed her one was waiting as he helped her into her coat and delivered her handbag.

## | LORNA RAE |

When Lorna Rae returned to the closet, it was late. She placed her on her side on the bench with her dust cover beneath her, making Lorna Rae feel like a small child being tucked into bed for the night. Once She had changed into her p.j.'s and hung up her clothes for the day and departed, the other bags peeked out from their shelves to inquire about the evening.

Lorna Rae was tired and not interested in engaging in any confrontations about the long day and the events at the apartment.

The Prada spoke first and asked about the night. Lorna Rae sighed and responded, "There is not much to report; the apartment was lovely, but I was placed in a closet with the coat by the butler and did not witness any conversations." Lorna Rae just wanted to call it a night. She felt guarded and protective of She at the moment, and she did not want to defend herself.

## | SHE |

She was tired, but her mind began to wander as she thought about the past few years. It was as if She knew in her bones that something was brewing to throw her life in another direction. It was like the sound of a train in the distance that you knew was approaching, but you had no idea how loud and scary it was going to be until it passed right by you, shaking you to the core. And now you were tied to the train tracks like an old time movie star screaming for help.

## Chapter Two

# A = ADVISE

*Ewan McGregor: "Can you keep a secret?"*
*Renée Zellweger: "Yes…"*
*Ewan McGregor: "Me too…"*
— Down With Love

She cuddled the Fendi beaded Baguette handbag tucked under her arm while she strolled down the cobblestone sidewalk on her way to the bistro in her neighborhood to meet her girlfriends for an emergency meeting to discuss the recent events of her career derailment and her future.

The beautiful beaded Baguette was another one of She's favorites; it was taken out on special occasions that didn't require many items due to its small size, or sometimes she used it as an everyday bag. The beads outlined small square floral designs with an accented exotic pink snake skin closure and straps, and tucked inside the yellow satin lining were the few necessities for an evening out: small Chanel wallet, cell phone, lipstick, tissue, and keys.

*The Baguette has its name because the shorter shoulder strap sits under the arm like a loaf of French bread. It was developed in 1997 by Venturini Fendi, who proposed creating a practical bag for women. She was quoted as saying, "It was the first bag that was treated like a garment. We made it in jeans, fur, leather, beads. The production was small, so the waiting list started, and the fever grew." British fashion writer Marion Hume described Baguettes as "beanie babies for grown-ups." Sophia Loren compared her penchant for collecting them to a drug addiction.*

The bistro was quiet for a Friday evening, but it would soon fill up and be loud with conversations. She found a corner table in the bar and was the first to arrive. One of her friends, who had arranged the meeting, invited two women who had at one point decided to change their lives completely; one had sold everything and moved to another country, and the other had moved across the U.S. She felt so blessed to have friends who cared enough to help her through this situation and to offer her alternatives and a fresh perspective.

Everyone arrived and settled in with introductions, and then the conversation started with a *Reader's Digest* version of She's history that led to her decision to leave and her future prospects. The other women told their stories, and She listened in amazement to their courage at taking such dramatic steps. They were good about asking She the right questions to narrow down the main issue, which was her job, not a change in location. They talked about vacations as part of the resolution in shaking things up and steering her in another direction.

The conversation took a bit of a turn when they started to contemplate the frustrations of some of corporate America and society in general.

"When did we become a working society of mediocrity? I am so tired of working with some people who think it's okay to do the bare minimum and then request the maximum in pay and benefits. Remember the days when we worked hard and didn't whine if we were given more responsibility? We took things on and were excited about making things better and more efficient. Now, some people are raising their kids to feel like everything they do deserves an accolade or award."

"Oh dear, we really are getting older when we sound like the two generations before us."

"Yeah, I don't know where we went wrong. I have taken classes on the different expectations of each generation, be it Baby Boomers, Gen X, and Gen Y, and I'm still confused as to what are appropriate expectations."

"Now there is a word, 'Expectations.' It can be overused as an answer to so many excuses. But maybe that's just me."

"You have to sit them down with a big smile on your face and use your inside voice to explain what they did wrong, or better yet, how you failed to give them better instructions. Ah yes, everybody gets a blue ribbon."

"That's brilliant—can I use this example at my next staff meeting?"

They all laughed at the silliness of it all. One of the women spoke up and challenged She to think about starting her own business. "I have to tell you," she said, "I went out on my own because I was running this large corporate office, and I have to say I got tired of babysitting."

"Oh my God, that is where I came from," She said. "I think as a manager, you can sometimes reach a point where you miss doing what you enjoy and are so distracted by trying to balance too many personalities and those who don't know how to work autonomously that it becomes too stressful and exhausting."

One of the women shared the story about a handbag: "It was stolen, and for months, I tried to find another like it to replace the one I loved so much. In the end, I couldn't find it because it was so unique, but I ended up finding another one I liked even more. Goes to show that sometimes when we run around trying to replace something we lost, what the universe is really trying to tell us is there is something better out there."

She listened intently, but she was horrified by the thought of losing any of her favorite handbags because they would not be easy to replace, especially given her current cash flow situation, and even though she had a good savings account, spending money on handbags was not part of the current plan. She reached next to her to make sure the Fendi was close, and she tucked it next to her in the booth so she could feel the weight of the beaded texture.

The story had also brought back the memory of the demise of one of her beloved handbags years earlier, during a ski vacation. She had placed the bag on the top of the car to free her hands to load some items in the backseat of the SUV, and she was distracted when they all got in the car, so she forgot to retrieve the bag. Well, it slipped off and the car ran over it, and once that was realized, in going back to fetch it, the car accidentally backed over it, which indeed killed the bag. What an unfortunate and messy death for a handbag. The bag had to be thrown away.

"Let's get down to the heart of the situation," said one of the women. "Now that we know you don't want to relocate, what do you really want to do, and how do you make that happen?"

"I have considered consulting, but that would require so much marketing on my part, which is not one of my strengths."

"Yeah, I agree. That's a tough one. How is your resume?"

"It's in pretty good shape but needs some tweaking. It's so different out there when it comes to looking for a job; everything is online these days, and you really do need to do the 100 cups of coffee theory—you know, where you need to make 100 coffee appointments as part of your networking."

"What about doing what you really love to do?"

This thought always stirred something in She—the fear of failure played a big part in keeping her from pursuing what she loved to do. She didn't know how to answer so she avoided the question. Her career had been such an important part of her life; she had never had the courage to make a change before. Maybe this was the universe pushing her in another direction. It gave her pause. What could she do? She so loved fashion and wished she had pursued a degree in the field. But life got in the way and things turned out differently.

The conversation about relocating and changing things up brought on a discussion about taking a trip to get away and experience new things.

"What city do you love? Where do you feel happy and want to go?"

"I so love Paris," She replied.

"Well, then you should go to Paris; there are direct flights and it's easy to go for a week or less just to get away."

What a fascinating thought! She was intrigued about such a spontaneous and impractical trip.

The reality of leaving her job was settling in. Subconsciously, She had felt it coming, but she didn't want it to end the way it did. One's career can sometimes be so wrapped into the definition of one's self that it becomes dramatic when things that are out of your control go wrong.

"I so appreciate you all taking the time to meet with me and discuss my options," She told her friends. "I am so fortunate to have friends who care."

The waitress came over with the checks. They paid their bills and said their goodbyes, and She promised to keep them posted on her progress.

## | FENDI |

At the bistro, the Fendi was nestled in beside She. A new Jimmy Choo was plopped down beside her and immediately struck up a conversation.

"Oh, what a day!" the Jimmy Choo said.

The Fendi responded, "What happened to you?"

"My owner was in a hurry this morning and placed a water bottle inside without the lid on tight enough, and it leaked all over my bottom. I feel like I wet my pants."

"That's terrible," said the Fendi. "Are you okay?"

"The good news is she noticed it by the time she got to work and was able to mop up the mess and clean me for the first time in months, so I do feel a little better."

"I guess with my size, that's something I wouldn't have to worry about. A water bottle would not fit."

"True," responded the Jimmy Choo.

The restaurant was getting loud, and they gave each other the look of "Oh, well, it was nice talking to you while it lasted."

Peeking under the tablecloth, the Fendi saw what appeared to be a Prada black backpack, made famous in the '90s due to its minimalistic design and industrial material, and stamped with a diminutive logo hanging from the back of the chair. The Fendi had met a few Pradas at the consignment shop she came from and was disappointed not to be able to meet this one. They were always so casual and easy to talk to.

The bags were not located in proximity to continue any further conversation, and as the evening came to a close, the Fendi wished drier days for the Jimmy Choo.

## | SHE |

Later that night, when She was home lying in bed, unable to sleep, the evening conversations went around in her head and the thought of a trip was very intriguing. She got out of bed and turned on her computer to research the expense of a trip to Paris. Just the thought of walking the streets, shopping, visiting museums, and sitting in a bakery enjoying C&C made her feel happy. She appeared to have enough miles to get a ticket, and now finding a place to stay required a little more research. She sent an email to a friend of hers who traveled a lot and would let others stay in her apartment while she was away. Then she sent an email to her two best girlfriends with the dates and flight schedule and let them know they might have a place to stay for free.

She was excited about the next chapter of her life, and She knew she needed to stay positive and work even harder to determine where she was headed. The rest of the week was filled with research online and reaching out to friends to network with; however, She knew it was probably a good idea to clean out her closet to produce some extra cash flow. Maybe starting a store on eBay to sell her designer clothes had the potential to keep the money coming in? Although from past experiences, the photographing of each piece, writing the descriptions, and dealing with the crazy questions from buyers was enough to convince She that an eBay store was not on the top of her list either. She would rather consign the items.

## | CLOSET |

The handbags knew something was up when She entered that morning and started to pull items from the closet, look at them intently, try some on, and then those that were chosen were placed on the rack she brought out for such cleanings. There were clothes she had not worn for a while or were similar to other favorite pieces. It was rare She got rid of items with regret, but there were a few She wished had not made it to the rack; the floral Prada pants were a little tight, but with the latest stress in her life, she had lost eight pounds, and now they would have fit perfect. She made a mental note to see whether she could locate them on eBay. There was also the Navy Gucci velvet cut blouse and the blue Balenciaga City handbag, but there could only be so many items in the closet, and if they were only hanging there, it didn't make sense to keep them. She then scanned the shelf of handbags and reached for the Dolce & Gabbana; it was a gorgeous bag but too heavy for her, so it needed a new home since she did not use it enough.

The group of bags all looked at each other at once when the Dolce & Gabbana left the closet, but nobody wanted to say anything. Those who had predicted its departure were especially silent, and the guilt of what they had said lay heavy on their consciences.

It was the Balenciaga City bag that finally spoke. "Well, we thought that might happen and we need to be prepared in case this should happen again. There is no sense turning on each other right now."

"Easy for you to say," said the group.

"Not really; if anything, I should be worried," said the City bag. "After all, I am not the first City bag in the closet, as I was so kindly reminded the other day, and it appears She has no problem recycling my kind."

They all grumbled. The tension of the situation was filling the closet like a dark cloud.

# | SHE |

It was another night at the favorite bistro on her street. She decided to dress up a little since she had been living in comfy cotton clothes the past few days of cleaning out every drawer and closet in her apartment to purge her life of any unnecessary things. She chose the wool Helmut Lang skirt, with tights, and a black Lanvin cashmere sweater with an amazing beaded neckline over a TSE cashmere tank. Topping it off with her Hermes wristwatch and diamond hoop earrings, She then selected her Lanvin pop clutch and matching Lanvin calf leather boots.

The night air was crisp as She strode efficiently and confidently down the busy sidewalk heading for the bistro. She could see the "Walk" sign lit in the next block. Cars rushed past. It was a busy Friday night and the Lanvin clutch that She purchased new at Nordstrom was tucked tightly under her arm as she passed characters on the sidewalk—semi-juveniles with their cell phones pasted to their ears or heads bent down while texting madly. *What a convenient, annoying society we have become,* She thought. All age groups were out for the evening; the young couples with friends, the older couples holding hands, clinging to each other as their world changed dramatically with each passing day. And, of course, the young single girls dressed up or came straight from work for drinks and whatnot.

She was again the first to arrive at the restaurant, which was small, cozy, and busy. She was lucky to find a four top in the bar and slid into the bench side of the booth.

She was meeting three of her best friends for dinner; two of them arrived shortly after her, and She stood up to greet them with hugs. They complimented her outfit and asked what she was wearing.

"I am almost entirely covered in Lanvin," She said, and she struck a pose saying, "Finally found a bag to match my shoes!"

They went on greeting each other with the usual "How are you?" and "What's new?" questions and finally ordered martinis and the conversation turned to men.

"Honestly, what does it take to find a good man these days?" one friend asked. "Do I need to dig a pit in my backyard and fill it with copies of the *New Yorker*, port, and Cuban cigars?"

"That's your selection?"

"Sure, why not. What kind of man do you want to attract? And feel free to insert the man of your dreams in this pit of despair."

"Wow, cynical party of one." A peel of laughter kicked in along with the martini's effect after a few sips.

"Okay, okay, my turn. How about *Sports Illustrated*, bicycle shorts, and a six pack of some fancy microbrew beer? If you are just trying to be realistic in finding a man, those are everywhere. Oh yeah, and by the way, the *Sports Illustrated* will be lying around the bathroom next to the toilet, along with the sweaty bicycle shorts. And don't forget empty beer bottles on your favorite coffee table—without a coaster."

"How about a true fantasy?"

"Well, if I wanted that, I would just throw George Clooney in there."

"Yeah, and jump in on top of him."

"Not me. I would pick Brian Williams…."

"Oh, that's a good one; he's dreamy."

"Or how about Jon Stewart?"

They all turned to the one who made that comment and stared in disbelief.

"What? He's so funny, and I think very handsome. I stand by my choice."

Their laughter filled the room, but hardly anyone noticed because the rest of the restaurant's volume had risen.

"All right, we are diverting from the game. You need to pick three things to attract an available and somewhat realistic man."

"Well, then it would be cable TV with all the sports packages, hiking gear, and his enormous financial portfolio."

By this time, the alcohol had kicked in and the restaurant owner had peeked around the corner to give the group the stink eye. They failed to see the facial scolding and continued with their game.

"Ha, my turn; I choose a toolkit because he needs to be handy."

"You mean handsy."

"Ha…a set of All Clad pans so he can cook, and lots of frequent flyer miles so we can travel."

"Good one. Okay, my turn. I would choose a nice tuxedo because I like to go to fancy events and dinners, etc., a Neiman Marcus credit card because he will love to take me shopping to buy me pretty things, and a copy of *Architectural Digest* for the perfect nest."

"You just described a gay man: a nice dresser who loves to shop and decorate…."

"Well, that wouldn't be so bad."

"Yeah and sanitary. Ha…Ha…."

"Okay, I have this dilemma; I'm dating three guys and need to narrow it down. At what point do I need to decide...?"

"If you're being a slut? Well, have you slept with any of them yet?"

"No."

"Well, then you are not a slut."

"But I made out with one of them the other night, and it was so nice. My face is raw from his five o'clock shadow burn."

"Really? What time was it?"

"Very funny."

"Besides, the one I'm really interested in wants me to make a decision."

"Yeah, and you can't very well keep hiding the extra flowers, dates, and rug burn either."

"It wasn't rug burn, beard burn."

"Potato, Patato."

Their one married friend finally joined them.

"Hey, how are you? Welcome back, and how was San Diego?"

"It was great. I am glad to be home; however, I miss the warm weather. I was going to stay longer because my husband wanted to spontaneously grab a flight to Hawaii for a few days. But the flight is so long; can you believe it?"

She responded jokingly, "No, you poor bitch."

"Very funny."

"I know; just kidding, my friend. Glad you are home. Do you want to order a drink?"

"It looks like I have some catching up to do."

The Friend ordered a martini and the evening was off and running. They didn't always have time to get together as often as they would like so this time together was precious and fun.

The Friend joined in with her funny stories of married life and told the group about one of her other married friends whose husband had been taking Lunesta to sleep; the wife woke up in the middle of the night to find him wide awake. They ended up having sex, and of course, he fell asleep right away. It was hilarious to hear her tell the story, and the way she giggled through the whole thing made it even funnier.

"If memory serves me, what man doesn't fall asleep right away?"

"Sounds like a naturopathic sleep aid; wonder why that is not being advertised."

"Yikes, can you imagine every night having to have sex just to get him to sleep? It's like giving a baby a bottle every night."

"Yeah, but you are the bottle."

### | LANVIN |

The Lanvin "Pop Bag" clutch, which was resting on the bench next to She, noticed when the conversation took a comical turn and that the group of ladies was having a marvelous time.

> *The Lanvin handbag is made of a soft calf leather with a toggle closure flap that covers a zipper pocket and the traditional coined fob that hangs from the pull with the Lanvin logo firmly stamped on each side of the coin.*

The Lanvin noticed the Prada Spazzolato tote, with a jewelry fob attached to the top, across the bench that belonged to an owner at the next table, so she decided to strike up a conversation.

"Hello, there. I can't help but notice your amazing jeweled accent; that is really cool."

The Prada smiled down at the Lanvin and thanked her and returned a compliment about the coin fob and her great condition.

"Thanks. I don't get out of the closet much so I really try to enjoy the moments like these when I meet someone new."

"I know what you mean; my owner has so many handbags, like a hundred, so we don't go out very often either, and some of us never leave the closet unless the owner gives us away."

"Wow, a hundred! How does that work? How do you fit in the closet?"

"This gal has an amazing closet, but some of us are really stuffed in pretty tight together. So you can imagine how nice it is to get out and breathe a little and enjoy the sites."

They both pondered this thought and looked around the restaurant, taking in the tasteful, elegant and comfortable décor, the white tablecloths, the unusual artwork, and the candles that illuminated each table. The clinking of glasses was barely audible over the conversations and especially the laughter coming from the Lanvin owner's table.

The next thing the handbags heard was one of the girls teasing one of the others.

"What is it with you and dogs? Every time one gets near you, it either piddles or pukes."

"Or they hump my leg. Remember when we went to your house and your dog came up and humped my leg. I said, 'Wow, that's the most action I've had in six months' right when your husband walked in. I never saw someone's face get red so fast, and he turned around and left the room."

"I know. Isn't he cute? So shy."

The Prada turned to the Lanvin. "Oh my, there is not enough mental sherbet in the world to cleanse my brain of that image."

The evening eventually came to a close and the Prada left a few minutes before the Lanvin. They wished each other the best and jokingly said, "Hope you get out again sooner rather than later."

### | SHE |

The car and driver were waiting outside her building when She came down that morning. The trip to her new friend's country estate had been arranged, and She was so looking forward to a long and relaxing weekend away from any sense of routine or memories of the past few weeks and her job situation.

The driver opened the door and politely took her wheeled luggage to place it in the trunk. She was carrying her Balenciaga City bag, which made her smile since she was headed to the country. The elegant casualness of the bag felt appropriate for the trip. Just enough room to carry what she needed in the car and the rest of her travel gear was in the luggage now, carefully stowed in the trunk of the town car.

She settled in the backseat, and as the driver pulled the car from the curb, he announced that the drive would take approximately two hours. There was bottled water in the backseat, so She helped herself and decided to take a few sips before resting her head and relaxing to enjoy the ride. Normally, She would be pulling out something to read and distracting herself for the trip's duration. Today, She felt like reflecting and looking out the window at the world outside. Before She knew it, the first bottle of water was gone and she knew she should probably pace herself so the driver would not have to pull over every thirty miles.

The car crept through the city from stoplight to stoplight and finally made its way to the freeway, passing industrial areas and then residential row houses that seemed to be stacked in line like the rows of Lego houses she had built as a child, feeling so limited by only the block-like structures with a few windows and a flat roof.

Before She knew it, the car exited to get onto the small two-lane road, and the scenery immediately changed to lush green trees and foliage. With each passing mile, the last few weeks seemed to disappear behind her. She let out a sigh and a smile crossed her face; it felt good to be in the car and enjoy the moment.

She sifted through her handbag, looking for the lip balm and a tissue, and then she found her cell phone to see that she had a text from a friend, inquiring about her whereabouts this weekend. She texted back that she was going out of town and would call when she returned.

She set the handbag on the seat next to her and closed her eyes to relax. She fell into a soft slumber that was interrupted an hour later when the car was jostled by a few potholes on the dirt road they were navigating. For a moment, She forgot where she was and felt frightened by what was happening, but before she could say anything, the car was on a beautiful paved driveway lined with thick trees, and the finely manicured landscape made it obvious they were nearing the Estate.

When the driver announced they would be arriving soon, She pulled out her mirror compact to check her makeup and make sure her mascara was not crumbling around her eyes after her short nap.

When she looked up, there was the house; it looked like a beautiful sixteenth-century chateau, and the front was dotted with floral trees creeping up the side and a few exterior potted urns overflowing with bright flowers.

She felt like she should have pulled up in a horse and carriage with a footman waiting to help her exit her coach. Instead, her hostess emerged from the front door, greeting her with a smile and waving from the elegant stone staircase.

"I'm so glad you are here," said the Woman. "How was the trip?"

The Woman's little dog was dancing at her feet and barked excitedly at the appearance of a visitor. And true to form, it piddled on She's Todd driving shoe.

## | CITY BAG |

The Balenciaga City bag was thrilled about being taken on a trip, but she was surprised when the town car did not head to the airport, but instead, was on the road for over an hour. At first, She held the bag in her lap and would go between letting it rest in her lap and fishing through the inside for lip balm and a tissue, and then checking her phone for any messages or emails. She finally set the bag next to her so it rested quietly on the seat while She dozed off for a nap.

The Balenciaga motorcycle City bag was originally developed in the 1990s by Nicolas Ghesquière, who became their creative director during that time period. The popular handbag comes in several colors and is made of soft, durable leather with its signature long leather tassels, hand-stitched handles, attractive silver tone accents, and centered exterior zippered pocket. It also has a zipper closure at the top and a removable shoulder strap along with an interior zip pocket, the Balenciaga engraved plaque, and a leather-framed hand mirror. Ghesquière's prototype was originally dismissed as too soft, too lightweight, and lacking in structure. However, these are the things that make the design so beloved. Ghesquière convinced the company to allow him to produce the bags just for the runway show so the girls would have something to carry while they walked, but the models were so in love with the design that it became a popular coveted bag.

# | SHE |

When they arrived, the City bag was scooped up as She exited the town car and was joined by the lovely hostess. She was escorted into the entry and the driver was behind her, bringing in the luggage and placing it in the entry. She handed him a tip before her friend could object, and he thanked her and was on his way.

The entry itself was a feast for the eyes, exhibiting old world elegance, but at the same time, a comfort that made you feel you could enter dressed in jeans or formal wear. She was wearing her favorite jeans, a cashmere sweater, a Dolce & Gabbana blazer, and Todd driving shoes. The Balenciaga was slung over her shoulder, and the pop of pink was a fun accent to the outfit.

She responded to her friend's question. "The drive was lovely—in fact I took a little nap, which I never do."

"Well then, this trip is just what you need, my dear," said The Woman. "Please come in and make yourself comfortable. Let me show you to your room and you can settle in, and then if it's okay with you, I can give you a quick tour and we can go for a walk in the garden. How does that sound?"

"Perfect," She responded, and they headed up the staircase to one of the many lovely bedrooms that had a fantastic view of the back of the house and garden area. The room had an adjoining sitting room and bathroom with a large tub. "Oh!" She exclaimed. "May I take a bath later? I love baths."

"Absolutely," the Woman responded and smiled. "It's one of my favorite things to do before bedtime. It makes for a good night sleep, don't you think?"

"Indeed," said She.

She then spent the next half-hour unpacking her clothes and setting out her toiletries in the bathroom. She changed into more comfortable slacks and walking shoes to tour the grounds, and She removed a Pashmina scarf from her bag to take with her.

She went downstairs and found her friend in the parlor lounging on one of the sofas.

"How about that walk?" asked the Woman.

"Sounds great," said She.

They spent the next hour walking through the gardens and stopped whenever She's hostess wanted to point out some of her favorite flowers and trees and how some of them were selected for the estate and their history. It reminded She of the times as a child when she would tour her grandmother's small garden around her tiny cottage, and the memory of those simple times brought her comfort.

After their tour of the grounds and the house, She retired to her room and changed into a nicer pair of wide leg pants and matching cashmere sweater. Slipping into a pair of velvet flats, She made her way down to the dining room to witness a beautiful table. Everything was done with such elegant details, from the table settings to the centerpieces, and of course, the food was amazing. The dinner, wine, and conversation went on until they both yawned at the same time and realized it was time to turn-in.

She's room was better than staying at The Plaza, and she melted into the soft bedding after taking a lavender bath. She drifted off into one of the most restful nights of her life.

The next morning, She awoke to the scent of crisp fresh country air coming from the window that She left slightly ajar. She stretched and wondered about breakfast; coffee sounded good. She forgot to ask what was the plan and did not know what the protocol was for staying in a private country estate. When She got up, she noticed a note had been slipped under her door that stated:

My dear, please dial 10 for the kitchen and they will bring you whatever you wish. I always sleep in on these mornings and you won't see me before 11. Make yourself comfortable and I will see you for lunch.

She was so pleased. This was exactly what she wanted—to have a quiet breakfast in her sitting area and read the book or fashion magazine She had brought with her, or just sip her coffee and enjoy the solitude and beauty around her. She called and ordered a pot of coffee, toast, eggs, and fresh fruit. It arrived on a silver platter, and She spent the morning lounging in the sitting room in a comfy robe she found in the bathroom, enjoying her breakfast, and she actually found herself humming when she was sipping her coffee.

The rest of the weekend was filled with relaxing activities, such as evening conversations in the living room with wonderful music in the background; they both had a love for Frank Sinatra, Dean Martin, and martinis. They took walks in the garden and a trip into town to walk through the farmers market where they selected fresh vegetables for dinner that night.

## | CITY BAG |

The Balenciaga spent most of the weekend curled up in a chair in the sitting room, basking in the sunshine that streamed in through the sheer drapes during the day. The pink bag only received attention that weekend when She needed to find her lip gloss or her book and magazine that were stuffed inside, and the bag was only taken out once on the trip to the farmers market.

## | SHE |

Sunday night came too soon, and She was whisked back into town to return to her reality of looking for a job. Her hostess tried to talk her into staying longer, but She knew it was time to get back to her life, and the trip to Paris was coming up.

# Chapter Three
# N = NEW

*Too much love will kill you just as*
*sure as none at all.*
— Queen

## | CHANEL BIARRITZ |

The Chanel Biarritz tote was sitting quietly on the chair in the airport and was unaware of anything amiss until it felt the small sticky hand patting around in a frantic fashion and touching nothing in particular—just anything the toddler could reach was the objective. Chanel was appalled and was hoping She would take notice and remove this obtrusive little person from her interior.

The canvas-leather tote with a zipper top and pockets on the side was ideal for travel, so She had tucked her dust-covered LV Murakami Cherry Pochette inside the

Balenciaga City bag and then inside the Chanel, so She had a few selections to choose from during her trip. The tote would spend most of the rest of the trip in the apartment, and the Pochette would see the sights of Paris, returning each night with stories to share with the tote.

*In 2007, the genius of Karl Lagerfeld proposed the Paris-Biarritz collection, which also offers a new concept of handbag, very different from the historical mood of Mademoiselle Coco because it is without the chain and with a different shape. The Biarritz handbag was inspired by the world famous holiday resort on the Basque coast of southwest France where Coco Chanel opened her boutique in 1915.*

Finally, She noticed the tot at the same time the mother did, and the intrusive little person was removed from the scene.

The tote felt better and was excited about taking a trip since She had not traveled on a plane for months. She then transferred the bag from the chair next to her and placed it on the floor between her feet to keep a better eye on it. She opened the bag and retrieved her book and the bottle of water from the side pocket and settled back to wait for boarding. Her travel companions were getting coffee and last minute purchases at the newsstand.

Chanel could now only see the parade of shoes walking by and the wheeled luggage passing through the corridors, and she was amazed by the variety of people you always find at an airport. There was the parade of pilots and flight attendants with their matching outfits and luggage, the elderly person being pushed in a wheelchair, the crying toddler in the stroller, those on vacation in their flip-flops, and of course, the business travelers always in a hurry. Chanel saw a woman walk by, carrying a Louis Vuitton tote, and it reminded her of the conversations in the closet with her roommates earlier that week when She was planning and packing for the trip.

## | CLOSET |

When the other handbags heard about the trip to Paris, they were all abuzz as to who would get to go. They were certain Chanel was going since her size and structure were appropriate for such a journey. The next question was who else would be included; there was always a smaller clutch and perhaps a mid-size bag. They were sure Lorna Rae would probably go, but Lorna Rae pointed out that she was not the type of bag conducive for a long trip or to be carried around the city all day while on vacation. This was why the smaller bags would be favored.

A few days before the trip, She entered the closet to start the packing process and started laying out outfits for each day and possible occasion. She pulled down the Tumi wheel luggage and Chanel tote from the upper shelf and scanned the rest of the handbags in the closet to see who should go. It made her envy those who used to travel with large steamer trunks filled with a wardrobe and every accessory. Nowadays, you had to consolidate and only take what was necessary, and She only liked to travel with carry-on luggage. The thought of her bag full of designer outfits running down the luggage ramps and being pawed through by strangers, or worse, disappearing altogether, was too much for her. You hear the stories about missing bags or items, and that's enough to make you sacrifice a few outfits for the comfort of knowing your possessions are safe and you will have something to wear when you arrive besides your travel togs.

She wished she could have also traveled during a time when people dressed up and it was an elegant event to fly. Now so many people look like they had just rolled out of bed before boarding that you didn't have to go much further with the cattle car description.

She reached for the Louis Vuitton Pochette in the red dust cover and placed in on the bench, and she then looked at the Lorna Rae, but she decided it would not travel well, and She wanted something that would not take up much room. The soft unstructured City bag was the obvious choice, and the pink color was fun since interjecting color was important. It seemed like travel clothes always ended up being black or darker colors for obvious reasons. That would be enough; besides, maybe she would buy a new bag as a memento from the trip. After all, it was Paris, the City of Love and Fashion, or her love of fashion—nice combo.

The phone rang and she left the closet. The City bag could hardly contain itself.

"I'm going to Paris. This is so exciting!" it exclaimed.

The other bags were envious. Lorna Rae was disappointed, but she knew the reasons why she was not sitting on the bench right now, so she accepted her fate of remaining home. The other bags also knew their chances were limited and tried to be happy for the City bag and Pochette.

"Make sure you pay attention and tell us everything you see when you return," they requested.

"Absolutely!" said the City bag.

The Chanel tote was happy about going too, but she knew her time would be spent as the pack mule to carry the other bags and necessities, and then she would more than likely remain in the apartment the rest of the trip unless an overnight or day trip was planned. The tote turned to Lorna Rae and started asking questions about the trip since she had probably witnessed more of the planning meetings.

"Do you know what the plans are for the trip? Do you think I will venture out beyond the airport and apartment?" asked the tote.

"I'm not sure, but I doubt it," said Lorna Rae. "Here is what I know; they have a direct flight and are staying at an apartment of a friend, and there was talk of the usual excursions of shopping, eating, and museums."

Lorna Rae went on to point out that City would probably join She for the day-long shopping trips while Pochette would be more likely to go out in the evenings and on museum trips.

The tote sighed and accepted her role.

Chanel said, "Well, I guess I will be the one carrying you along unless she crams you in the wheeled luggage."

"Oh, I hope not; that sounds claustrophobic," said the Pochette.

"I've done it before," the Lanvin said, "and it's not so bad as long as you're tucked inside your dust cover and not on top of anything, like a pair of heels poking in your side."

She had finished her phone call and was back in the closet. She spent the next half-hour trying on outfits and doing her best to consolidate and find interchanging outfits to cut back on the amount of clothes she needed to take. Since this was Paris, there had to be few pieces that stood out. She picked out some basic Jil Sander and Prada slacks and TSE sweaters and went with a colorful Etro coat to tie it all together. Now the shoes were always a dilemma when traveling because they had to be comfortable for walking and look good. She pulled out her Todd flats and a pair of low heel Prada boots and one pair of Manola Blahnik embellished pumps that would work for an evening out. Along with the undergarments, p.j.'s, and a few other layering pieces, that would be enough.

## | CHANEL |

*Going through security is always such a treat,* Chanel thought sarcastically, as she was opened and the toiletries and laptop inside her were inspected. *Being pushed and shoved down a conveyor belt and forced to enter a dark cavern only to be spied upon and x-rayed; now this cannot be healthy,* Chanel thought, all the while hoping the machine did not stop to dwell on her contents. Fortunately, today she proceeded through security without any issues. *It's like going through a mini-carwash without all the soap and water*, thought Chanel, although she felt dirty coming out to the daylight on the other end. *I could use a good Handi Wipe about now.*

The plane ride was rather uneventful, although the Chanel tote found the ride rather miserable and looked forward to a quiet week in the Paris apartment after being stuffed under the seat in front of She. Chanel had to endure the long flight next to a Tumi zippered tote that would not shut up. She glanced across the aisle at the Louis Vuitton tote and they both gave each other a knowing look of "Are you kidding me? How much longer can this go on?"

Chanel turned to the Tumi and said, "That is so interesting, but if you don't mind, I had a harrowing security experience, so I could use a nap." It was a little white lie, but she needed a break. Instead, it was like adding fuel to the fire; the Tumi showed concern but went on to describe an experience she'd had a few years back when her owner went through security and got pulled aside because something showed up on the screening. Come to find out it was something on the handle of the bag, and more than likely in the hand lotion her owner had put on earlier. They were delayed and almost missed their flight. Chanel could not have been more bored and was so disappointed that on her trip to Paris she was stuck next to this non-stop talker with the most uninteresting stories to tell. The bag wished she could hop across the aisle and talk to the Louis Vuitton, who seemed just as bored with her travel mate—a worn-out backpack that smelled of cigarette smoke.

## | SHE |

She arrived later that evening at the gorgeous apartment. She and her travel companions were so thankful the key was left in the urn atop the pedestal table in the hallway as promised. She pulled off the top and reached in, and they all looked at the key at once; it was the shape of a skeleton key, and being thankful it was there made them all smile and they broke into giggles.

They made their way through the apartment, found the bedrooms, and agreed to call it a night; they would not hold each other to a schedule the next morning for breakfast. They had traveled enough together that they seemed to be able to navigate any new city or place with ease.

In the morning, they all seemed to get up within an hour of each other and were in the kitchen finding their way around to make coffee and start a list of items to pick up at the market for the week. One of the girls had gone out earlier and found a bakery, and she had come back with a bag of fresh pastries and a baguette; she had also picked up some fresh fruit and cream for the coffee. They ate their breakfast while hovering in the kitchen and sitting at the small breakfast table; they were all telling funny stories and talking about what to do that day.

She said, "Did I tell you about the time I came here last fall and stayed with my friend, Brigid, who works for *Vogue*?"

"No," they said, all turning in curiosity to hear the story about to unfold.

"Well, Brigid had this cute little Yorkie dog, and I couldn't figure out why it would not listen to any of my commands while Brigid was at work; you know, 'Sit. Down. Here, girl…' It took about two days, and then I figured out the dog only understood French. From then on, she obeyed the commands. Who knew…?"

They all laughed.

"I have one too," said her friend. "My neighbor had this dog, Charlie, that used to roam the neighborhood because everyone's property was so large and located outside of town. One day the dog wandered over to the neighbor's house, and the owner called the neighbor and said, 'Is Charlie there?' 'Yes,' they responded. 'Well, put him on the phone.' They obliged and put the phone up to the dog's ear and the owner said, 'Charlie get home.' And the dog took off and went home."

"Are you kidding me?"

"That can't be true."

"I swear it's a true story."

"I have one," the other friend said. "I was at this dinner party last year and we all put our handbags in the hostess' bedroom. Well, her little Bison Fiche dog went into the room and got into almost all the handbags and chowed down on anything edible like crackers, candy, etc. and then proceeded to wander into the kitchen and throw up. What a mess it made in the bedroom too!"

"Ick! Makes you always want to have a bag with a zipper closure."

"Dogs are so funny."

"I really want to go shopping today," said She. "I can't wait to just wander into Chanel and go to each floor dreaming of a new wardrobe, and, of course, stop by Dior to see the handbags."

"I think I want to go to the Louvre museum and wander."

"I hate to say it, but I am so jet-lagged I just want to hang out here, and take a long hot bath, and read my book on the patio, and maybe wander around the neighborhood later."

"Okay, let's meet back here and decide what to do for dinner."

"Agreed."

She got ready that morning and the shower felt so good. It was nice not having to hurry to be anywhere—that's what a vacation is all about. Lounging around that morning with her girlfriends and enjoying breakfast was fabulous, and now having a lazy morning to get ready and head to Chanel was a dream come true. She took her time getting ready and selected a pair of Jil Sander slacks and sweater and the Etro coat and Todd flats, and she took the little Louis Vuitton Pochette in order to travel light. As long as she had her credit cards and a city map, she was set. At the last minute, she changed her mind and grabbed the City bag and added a few more items to the pink Balenciaga bag so she could take more with her since she would be gone most of the day.

On her way out the door, She reminded her friends, "Okay, last one out, drop the key in the urn. Oh, by the way, there isn't a peephole for security. In case anyone arrives later and we need a password, how about 'The rooster crows at midnight,' or no, how about, 'Ex-lax is not chocolate?'"

"Ewww."

"Well, the other is so obvious."

"Yeah, but can we pick something not so juvenile?"

"I love Lanvin."

"That works."

"Very funny. I don't think we need a password, paranoid Patty. I would think we can recognize each other's voices by now."

"You never know; your drunk voice is a little deceiving."

"Oh, that's hilarious coming from you."

"Hey, I thought it was very clever."

"See you tonight, and let's find a fun place for dinner. I'm in the mood for wine and gorgeous French men."

"I know just the place," said She. "I will stop by it when I am out and make reservations for 7 p.m."

"Sounds fabulous; have fun and don't come home unless you buy something wonderful to share with the rest of us."

"You wish!"

She pulled out the map to get her bearings and headed for the Metro to catch the train that brought her to the closest stop to Chanel and her next destination, Dior. She loved to go shopping by herself—to take her time looking at what she wanted and not have to be on anybody else's schedule was ideal. Shopping in boutiques, each designer shop is a sea of luxurious handbags and a feast for the eyes: Chanel, Lanvin, and Dior—oh my!

She's feet felt like they were floating as she rushed up the stairs from the Metro, her legs moving quickly beneath her; she could not get to the store fast enough. Her heart rate quickened as she got closer and came around the corner that revealed the shrine that was Chanel. Entering the store was always such a heady experience, and She stopped for a moment to take a deep breath and inhale the beauty and history that surrounded her. She was greeted by a salesperson and could not help but notice the security guard at the front door. She moved quietly from floor to floor to take in the art before her, and she reached out only occasionally to touch the fabric and check the price on some items. Coats were always her weakness, so she tried on a few and smiled at her reflection in the mirror as she turned around slowly to take it all in and then gently hung the garment back on the velvet hanger.

The costume jewelry counter was one of her favorite places to shop, and more within her budget, so she was hoping to find a piece to take home with her. She found a place to sit at the counter and placed her Balenciaga next to her as she scanned the case and wished she could afford one of the many classic pearl necklaces, but she could not afford a luxury like this even if she had a job at the moment. There were so many pieces to choose from, and she was tempted to buy earrings, but what she really thought would go with so many pieces was a beautiful broach in pastel stones, so she selected the piece to purchase.

Her next stop was Dior and then Lanvin, one of her favorite designers. When she didn't find anything else to buy, she decided lunch was in order. She found a café and ordered a sandwich and coffee and settled into a corner table to observe the patrons around her.

She looked across the Paris café and found herself analyzing each woman's handbag and the story behind it. There was a young woman, sitting at the next table, who was talking wildly in French on her phone in a somewhat hushed tone that was distracting, but it was the state of the woman's handbag that caught She's attention. It was a gorgeous black Hermes 42cm Birkin Bag; however, it was being used as what She could only analyze as a wastebasket. From where she was sitting, she could see the woman searching through the bag for something, and then the woman proceeded to empty some of the contents on the table. There was, of course, the overstuffed wallet, a bottle of water, numerous receipts, and miscellaneous papers that looked like notes of some kind, makeup (not in a separate zipper pouch—horrors), tampons, a pack of cigarettes, a lighter, and a small item of clothing that appeared to be a cashmere shrug. Even after the woman stopped emptying the contents and found the item in question, She could visualize the bottom of the bag littered in loose change, bits of tobacco from the cigarettes, and a lip gloss missing its cap and oozing into the soft leather lining. All of a sudden, the bag slipped from its owner's lap and landed on the floor. It landed with a soft thud, and She winced when it fell. Without stopping her conversation, the woman picked it up and set in on the chair next to her. Then the woman stooped down to gather the few items that fell out of the bag and shoved them back into it.

She wished someone was there with her to witness the crime, and cluck and whisper about such an atrocity, and, of course, do it in French. It made her laugh inside at the thought of such snobby assumptions. Her feet were already tired after her morning shopping, so she decided to get another cup of coffee, and have a coconut macaroon, and enjoy her afternoon of people judging. *Can't really call it people watching after my last judgmental observation*, She thought.

She spent the rest of the afternoon wandering around the Place Vendome section of Paris, but she decided not to overdo her first day. After sitting on a bench for a few moments to check her Metro map, it was time to head back to the apartment and relax a bit before heading out to dinner. On her way back, she stopped at the restaurant near the apartment and made the reservations for dinner as promised.

## | LOUIS VUITTON POCHETTE |

The next day, She planned a trip to the Musee Galliera fashion museum, and this time, she took her little Louis Vuitton Mukasi Pochette. She knew it was the kind of collector bag with its two cheerful cherries on the front that made people take notice and comment on the fun artwork donning the bag's exterior.

*In 2004, Takashi Murakami, a famous Japanese artist and founder of the "Superflat" movement, created the "Cherry Blossom" pattern, in which smiling cartoon faces in the middle of pink and yellow flowers were sporadically placed atop the "Monogram Canvas." This pattern appeared on a very limited number of pieces that sold out quickly. Murakami followed this popular and coveted line with the "Monogram Cerises" pattern, in which cherries with faces on them were placed over "Monogram Canvas." The line was sold on LVMH's official retail website, eLUXURY, in the spring of 2006, but by the end of May 2006, it was no longer available.*

The little bag liked these types of outings when it was just the two of them, and going to the museum was amazing. Later on that day, they were sitting at a café having espresso when the Pochette noticed another handbag at the next table that was sitting on the ground. It was so overloaded, bulging with possessions and obviously uncomfortable, that it was barely able to speak. The seams were stretched and threads popped, and it was scuffed and stained. It seemed such a contradiction that a bag like this would be wandering the streets of Paris. However, when the Pochette noticed the owner of the bag, with her tennis shoes and khaki shorts and T-shirt with a slogan, the Pochette knew the owner was not a Parisian woman.

The bag thought about her history and was so happy to be part of her current family. She had purchased the bag on eBay and Pochette remembered how her former owner kept her in her original box and dust cover on the shelf. It was like Pochette belonged to some nerd who kept his Star Wars figurines in their original packaging to hold their value and never played with them. For the Pochette, her life changed when she arrived on She's doorstep in the little postal box, finally to be unwrapped and enjoyed. She took her out of the box and out into the world. *And now, look at me,* the Pochette thought, *sitting in Paris enjoying the sights and sounds of one of the most beautiful places on the planet we call Earth.*

# | **SHE** |

She and her traveling companions selected a bus trip and to stay overnight in Versailles as their only excursion that week. When they pulled up to the immense estate, it took She's breath away. It did every time she saw it. The opulence and beauty of the chateau's gardens and parks made her want to weep. With the chateau's 2,153 windows, 700 rooms, and 67 staircases, She felt right at home and wanted to go back to Paris to fetch the rest of her luggage and move-in. *Do you think anyone would notice?* She laughed to herself. She pictured herself in a formal gown, wandering through each drawing room and ending up in the Hall of Mirrors. With each step, her dress would rustle and swish across the marble floors with only a tiny click of her fabulous heels. What a marvelous fantasy!

The day was filled with the walking tour through the palace and gardens. They then went into town to find their tiny but chic hotel, and then they spent the rest of the day wandering the cobblestone streets, taking in the small shops and admiring the architecture of the town, especially the different doorways that you wished could tell the story of each of their occupants over the years.

The next morning, it was back to Paris to make the most of the rest of the week that was quickly coming to an end.

She decided to go for a walk along the Champs-Élysées one day, and she took along the Pochette since it was just for a casual stroll to take in the sites and people watch. The streets were heavy with traffic that day, and everyone seemed to be in a hurry. It felt like a contrast to the expectation and wonder of Paris. It didn't bother her that much because it felt glorious just to be in her favorite city and have nothing scheduled to do but wander. As she came around the corner of a small narrow cobblestone street, there appeared to be a high fashion photoshoot going on. It was interesting to watch how efficient the photographer was with setting up the shot, and the model was comfortable making her contortionist poses. There was only a photographer, his assistant, and the model. They were not the least bit phased about She stopping to watch their work, and before She knew it, they had packed up their equipment and were moving to what she could only assume would be their next location. The lanky model strutted behind them like an elegant giraffe.

She wondered what it would be like to have the nomadic and gypsy lifestyle of a fashion model. The thought of going on interviews to get the job, and all of the rejection and hearing someone judge your figure openly sounded stressful. Having to go on locations and stand around for hours while the shots are being prepared—maybe it was not as glamorous as it appeared. But getting to wear such lovely clothes sounded like fun.

On her way back to the apartment, She came across a small flea market and found each booth more fascinating than the last. There were books, furniture, knickknacks, and antiques. She wondered what were the stories behind all of the discarded objects and whether they would find new homes or they would continue to be peddled every day only to be tossed out in the end.

A small table in the corner of the market displayed a case housing vintage jewelry. It was fascinating to see all the lovely pieces, and a pair of unique delicate chandelier earrings caught She's eye. She bartered with the owner of the wares and was able to get a good price for the pair.

꧁◈꧂

They were sitting at the restaurant and consuming their first bottle of wine when She looked across the room and noticed an extremely handsome man. In fact, it seemed like most of the men around them were quite good-looking and well-dressed.

"You know," She said as she poured her second glass of wine, "we need another bottle, and have you noticed how gorgeous the men are here?"

They all took a moment to pan the room and then nodded in agreement.

"Oh, dear," said her friend. "I feel a game coming on."

"Indeed, you do…. Okay, here it is. See the guy at the bar? The one who looks like a cross between John Stamos and Rob Lowe?"

"Yeah," they all said at the same time while trying not to stare.

She leaned in, and they all did too, as she lowered her voice to start the game.

"Okay, if he were your man, what one thing would you tolerate or sacrifice to make it so? And keep in mind for this exercise that he is the perfect man."

"I'll go first…"

"Wait a minute; how would you describe the perfect man?"

"That's a whole other game, so let's just focus on this," She said jokingly.

"If he were my man, I would let him watch golf all day and not complain."

"If he were my man, I would pretend to enjoy spending the holidays with his crazy family; you know they are always crazy."

"If he were my man, I would rub his back every night."

"Wait a minute; that doesn't sound like a sacrifice; he's so gorgeous how could you not have your hands on him every night?"

"If he were my man, I would be willing to go camping. Oh yeah, out in the woods with him wouldn't be so bad."

"If he were my man, I would listen to his stories about his baseball card collection and appear to be fascinated."

"If he were my man, I would never complain if he left the kitchen cabinet doors open. And for a bonus round, he could even leave the toilet seat up."

"What is up with that? Do all men have an aversion to shutting a cupboard door?"

"Maybe they are trying to be efficient because they will be getting back in it again."

The game lost steam as they consumed more wine and the man of the moment departed the restaurant.

"Well, there he goes."

"And there goes our fun."

It was a perfect evening of good food, wine, and conversation, and so relaxing. Dining in Europe was such a wonderful experience of truly enjoying the meal and not putting any time constraints on departing.

As they headed down the street and back to the apartment, they were taking their time and soaking up the sights of the neighborhood and the twinkling lights that are Paris. Somewhere in the distance, you could hear a dog barking and the squeak of a tiny car horn. It sounded like a large dog's chew toy. They burst out laughing when they heard it.

# Chapter Four
# D = DESTINY

*Jane Russell: You think you're so smart.*
*Keenan Wynn: No, I think you're that stupid.*
— The Fuzzy Pink Nightgown

Arriving back at home, She crossed the threshold, dragging her wheeled luggage, two shopping bags, and her Chanel tote. Paris was so wonderful, but it felt good to be home. She went about her usual routine after a trip and unpacked, started laundry, and went through the small stack of mail.

As she unpacked and put away toiletries and made laundry and dry cleaning piles, she carefully unwrapped the Pochette and City bags from their dust covers and used a damp washcloth to remove all the travel dust and germs they might have picked up. She always did this after traveling, and she made sure the wheeled luggage and Chanel got a good sponge bath before they were put away. It was a routine with her, and recently, she had read an excerpt from a magazine that talked about how many germs can accumulate on your handbag. The comparison the magazine made was that there are more germs there than on a public toilet seat. Gross; all the more reason for the wipe down.

## | CLOSET |

After the bags had been cleaned and tucked in for the night, and after She had departed, the chatter started. The handbags waited until they knew it was safe after She had gone to bed and the closet was dark. Then they all chimed in at once.

"How was the trip? We want to know everything. Don't leave anything out."

The three travel companions looked at each other.

"Well, who should go first?" asked the Chanel tote.

The YSL hopped to the end of the shelf, wanting to get closer, even though the Chanel was directly across the room on an upper shelf of the closet.

The Chanel continued. "As you can imagine, I was the pack mule for the trip, and the flight over was so miserable with this yackety-yak Tumi tote next to me that would not shut up. Anyhow, the apartment they stayed in was marvelous, and I was there the whole time, except I did get to go on an overnight trip to Versailles and that was quite fun."

"Did the rest of you go?"

"Nope, just me," said the Chanel.

"What did she use for a handbag?"

"She just tucked her small Chanel wallet in the inside of her coat pocket."

"So tell us about the getaway?"

Chanel went on to describe the trip; however, she was stowed until they went to the hotel so she only got a glimpse of the estate.

## | SHE |

She met one of her best friends at their favorite restaurant, and when she arrived, it was so busy that they could not find a table and had to sit at the bar. Fortunately, there were hooks underneath to hang their handbags. There was nothing worse than trying to find a place to put your handbag while sitting up on a barstool. You couldn't place it on the bar—not enough room—and putting it on the back of the chair was not safe, and placing it behind you on the barstool was uncomfortable. She had to make sure the gentleman sitting next to her did not mind that she hung it between them since it encroached into his space.

They ordered drinks and dinner and settled into the banter of catching up on their week. At one point, her friend turned to her and said, "I was just wondering why everyone at the bar was staring in our direction, and I thought, 'Hey, we must look pretty good tonight,' and then I noticed that the TV is above our heads and they are watching the baseball game."

## I LORNA RAE I

There were now two handbags under the bar, dangling from their hooks. The Celine studded clutch turned to Lorna Rae and said, "Hey, you hang out here often?"

Lorna Rae glanced in her direction and couldn't help but laugh. "Not much, but the view is interesting, wouldn't you say?"

"Yeah, fortunately my owner wore pants tonight; nothing worse than looking up a skirt from this angle or getting jabbed by knobby knees."

## I SHE I

It was Saturday morning and She was headed to her favorite consignment store. It felt good to be back to her usual routine. She decided to go fancy and comfortable and was wearing black leggings, a Lanvin black satin dress, an Etro cardigan sweater, Prada platform sandals, and carrying the beaded Fendi.

When She walked in the door, she was immediately attracted to the selection of handbags placed in the cases, and she scanned the shelves to see whether anything caught her attention enough to make the investment. She had purchased and consigned so many bags over the years that finding one to add to her closet was a rare occasion. Some of them were too big for her, and others were not the right style or color or had too much hardware. Every now and then there would be the Goldilocks of handbags that was just right—like the Fendi she was carrying today or her Prada that had been purchased at this same shop. Sometimes, there would be a Hermes or Chanel, but their price range was still too rich for her blood to justify the expense. But it was always fun to dream. Today there was a great selection, but nothing seemed to catch her eye. After greeting the owner and catching up on the highlights of her trip to Paris, She settled into scanning the clothes and shoe racks for any deals she couldn't resist. Today was a major score when she found a pair of brand new, never been worn, Manola Blahnik satin sling backs with mink fur accents. They fit perfectly and would look so cool with slim leg pants or rolled up jeans. She bounced out of the shop, excited to get home to find a place on her shelf for the new shoes and to try them on with a few outfits.

## | FENDI |

As they approached the consignment shop, Fendi was wondering whether she would see any of the bags that were at the store during her short stay before coming home with She. When they came through the door, Fendi scanned the shelves immediately and noticed that the Gucci she had sat next to was still there, along with a Bottega Veneta Intrecciato Nappa handbag.

## | SHE |

The job search was more tiring and stressful than She had imagined. Just researching how to interview well and answer the questions was exhausting. *How do you answer the one about "What are your weaknesses?" Ugh..who likes that one?* She thought. *Let's see, my weakness is not being able to tolerate a toxic work environment for more than eight months—no, how about my weakness is expecting too much from my employees? That's probably a flaw more than a weakness. How about my weakness is wanting to scream at colleagues who show up late and spend half their day socializing. They probably wouldn't like any of those. Can't be negative. Although what fun it would be just to say what you think at work for one day without any consequences. That would be a good SNL sketch; come to think of it, that's the premise of the whole show. No wonder it has such a large audience; watching people say and do things we all wish we could do without consequences.*

Now She was staring at her reflection in the mirror in front of her desk in the bedroom and tapping the pencil on her lip, deep in thought. *Hmm...should have done my hair today instead of just pulling it back in a ponytail and maybe put some makeup on. Not feeling very groovy today.* She was also thinking about the strange dream she'd had the night before where she was walking with a crowd of people through a large building like an airport, but the floors were wood and different colors, and all of a sudden, sections of floor were opening up and people were dodging the gaps to keep from falling in so she was looking at her feet, watching her step, and stopped to avoid falling, but then she noticed the ceiling was closing in. She turned around to go in the other direction to try and avoid both issues, and for some reason, her former boss was there and he turned around, also going in the other direction, and disappeared. She kept calling his name, but he didn't come back. She analyzed the dream as a way of dealing with her sudden departure from her job and how she felt so betrayed. But her boss was not the one who had betrayed her; others had let her down, and unfortunately, he could not stop the train that ended up running her off the tracks.

It was a gray day outside, perfect for staying in and trying to get something accomplished in her research. The rain falling against the windows made a romantic swooshing sound. She drew open the window and took in a deep breath. She was still in her bathrobe, which seemed to match her hair and makeup situation. Being alone and needing to communicate, she talked aloud, "I wonder if I would feel more successful if I dolled myself up a bit; maybe not, too late in the day. Think I will curl up in bed and watch an old movie. I can do more research tomorrow." Feeling a little cold, she wandered into the closet to get some socks. "Oh, all my pretty clothes, we need to take a field trip from this dismal day." *Wow, crazy party of one.*

She ended up shedding the robe and comfy clothes and opened the framed glass doors in the wardrobe that held her formal gowns. She pulled out the red Calvin Klein strapless structured gown and slipped it on along with the matching color Armani formal pumps. She combed and pulled her hair back and brushed on a little blush and lipstick; she admired her reflection in the full-length mirror in the master bathroom. She found the beaded Natalie Wood bag and strutted around the closet like she actually had someplace to go. She looked down at the bag and sat on the bench in the closet. It made her contemplate the life this bag must have had. She wondered whether it had once gone to glamorous parties, or did it end up forgotten in the closet? Next up was the fitted L'Wren Scott black cocktail dress along with the Chanel platform heels. She looked in the mirror and let out a "Meow." *Hello, Kitty! I may be getting too old for this look.* She took off the dress and put on a pair of YSL tuxedo pants and an Etro cashmere sweater and topped it with a fur short jacket and a chunky Lanvin rhinestone necklace; now that looked more appropriate, fun, and elegant. She then decided on a cashmere pant and sweater set to spend the rest of the day in. She hung up the rest of the clothes from her spontaneous fashion show and went to the kitchen to fix a cup of coffee and spend the rest of the evening hanging out on the couch reading her fashion magazines and watching a movie.

The next day, She pulled herself out of the slump She had fallen into and made appointments for coffee every morning that week as part of her networking. The meetings all went well, but her confidence was waning, and it took all her strength to keep her attitude up that week. Her last appointment on Friday was with her headhunter, and he did not have a very rosy outlook for her. The problem was there were not many opportunities in her advanced career state, so it might be time for her to strike out on her own with her own business. It was something she had contemplated before, but the thought of starting over at her age was a little scary.

It's always when you least expect it—the call came in and She received an offer for a three-month consulting job at a firm she had always admired and for which she wanted to work. She made arrangements to meet with the VP and felt good about this new prospect.

## | CLOSET |

It was quiet in the closet that day, like most days. Suddenly, YSL looked up and noticed small beads of water coming down the wall.

"Hey, do you see that?" she asked the Prada sitting next to her.

"Yeah, that's strange; I wonder where it's coming from?"

They exchanged a look and wondered about this new phenomenon and whether it would get worse or stop.

The other bags soon were alerted and they all began to talk at once.

"I don't mind being rained on now and then, but if something breaks and a lot of water comes through, that would be scary."

"I don't like being rained on."

"Well, hello, Miss High Maintenance, you little closet body."

"Cute, but I don't want my leather exterior to get damaged."

The water was coming down a little faster, so it made them scoot away from the area.

"Well, now what do we do? Is She home and how long until someone notices this interior fountain?"

The water was starting to pool on the top shelf where YSL was sitting and she started to whine a little more.

"Oh, this is terrible; it's starting to touch my corner."

"Try and move yourself out of the way and use something else to block the water."

YSL looked around, noticed a tiny stack of shoe dust covers behind her, and pushed them toward the tiny pool forming on the shelf.

"There, that should hold it for a while."

She came in the closet to pick out a jacket and shoes before leaving. The handbags felt relief, thinking the leak would be discovered, but She was in such a hurry that she did not look up and notice the trickle coming down the wall.

Once She was gone, the handbags broke into a slight panic.

"Well, now what? How long will she be gone this time, and how much longer do we have until something terrible happens?"

"Ahhhh, there is another leak over here," said the Chanel tote, which was stored in the upper shelf on the other side from the YSL.

"Quick, slip off your dust cover and use it to protect yourself. Or, use one of the shopping bags to absorb some of the water."

She came back a little later, and when she turned on the light, she saw the glistening water coming down in two parts of the closet and let out a squeal. "What the hell is this?" She scrambled to move the bench near the side of the closet next to the shelf. Then she reached up to rescue the bags, and in a panic, she tossed them to the ground. She felt the saturated dust covers and then hurried to the bathroom to grab some towels to mop up the water that had pooled on the shelf. After soaking up the water with the two towels, she removed them along with the wet dust covers, tossed them into the tub, and then grabbed two more towels to mop up the mess. Next, she rushed to the bedroom, where Lorna Rae was lying on the bed. She grabbed the handbag, searching for her cell phone so she could call the building manager and get someone to respond to the water leak.

The YSL, Prada, and Chanel all lay on the closet floor, moaning.

"Oh, that hurt. Did she have to toss us down like that?"

"Guess it beats getting soaked."

"I don't know. I wonder how long it would have taken me to dry out."

"Crap, I landed right on my handle. Ouch!"

The next week involved scheduling a contractor to come in and repair and paint the wall after the leak was fixed. She moved the handbags and some of the clothes out of the way so the workers could repair the wall, and she had them drape the rest of the closet in plastic to avoid any damage.

When the workers showed up, She was disappointed that one of them reeked of cigarette smoke, and she was hoping they would finish quickly before her entire closet was polluted with the scent. She should have known better and made sure to request smoke-free workers. This situation had happened before, but She had forgotten to ask the manager. For now, She was as polite as possible, and fortunately, the workers were only there for two hours. Once they left, She sprayed air freshener in the closet and opened the bedroom window in hopes the stench would dissipate quickly.

The bags were piled in the hallway, all lined up like soldiers, while the closet was being repaired and painted, and the smell of the paint and one of the stinky workers filled the apartment—such a strange toxic combination. Even after She sprayed the closet to remove the smell, the handbags remained in the hallway until the next day. The bags were so close together that they were getting on each other's nerves, due to the inconvenience of the work going on in their nest.

"Do you have to poke me with your handle?"

"Do you always have to complain?"

"Will you just move over a little?"

"Well, I can't, so just relax."

"When will they be done already? I hate being on the floor in the hallway, and yesterday She accidentally kicked me and knocked me over when she went by in such a hurry."

"I just want to go back to my shelf so I can rest and see what's going on from my perch."

Their quarreling was a true sign that these little high maintenance handbags, like high maintenance ladies, don't like change or disruption to their usual routine.

The situation reminded them of one of Longchamp's stories of riding in the car when there had been one of those rare mishaps when the car slowed down suddenly and Longchamp got catapulted to the floor; inevitably, her contents were sprayed on the passenger side floor mat. The experience had been so traumatic that Longchamp was still shaking after they returned home, and she was placed back on the shelf in the closet. When the bag relayed the story to the rest of the group, they listened in horror; only a few of the other bags had ever witnessed such an event.

*In 1948, Jean Cassegrain inherited his family tobacco shop and he designed a leather-covered pipe that became a popular luxury item. He picked the name Longchamp because he would walk by a horse race track in Paris that was called Longchamp, translating to "long field," and he felt that would be a good name for his company. The company is still owned and managed by the family and is primarily known for its leather and canvas handbags and travel items. The Roseau Croco crocodile-style full-grain leather handbag is both chic and trendy.*

"It happened so fast," Longchamp said, now remembering it, "that She was unable to catch me before I landed on the car floor. Some of the contents flew out of my top and were scattered and rolled around on the floor until She arrived home and was able to scoop everything up and plop it back inside me. Then my interior felt clumpy as all the contents were jostled about in a disorganized manner. She was in a hurry and did not have time to place the items carefully. When we arrived home, She removed all the items and wiped down my exterior with a soft damp cloth to remove any dust from landing on the floor. Then I felt better, but I was happy to be back on the shelf and tucked in my dust bag."

## | SHE |

She was invited to dinner at the Four Seasons with her lovely new older friend. She was looking forward to catching up since last seeing her friend at the Country Estate, and She had only been able to exchange a few phone conversations to let the Woman know about the trip to Paris and the job search.

She loved having dinner at a Five Star Hotel because it felt like she was traveling in style even though she was home.

"You look so good tonight, as always," said the Woman. "What are you wearing?"

"Well, the suit is Dolce & Gabbana, the top is Missoni, the boots are Gucci, and my coat is Lanvin, and the handbag is YSL," She replied.

"Oh, heavens, can I get a broom and dustpan to sweep up all those fancy designer names?" asked the Woman.

"You're one to talk; look at you in the gorgeous Chanel suit and carrying a Birkin. Well, I knew since we were going out to a fancy restaurant, I should dress fancy."

"Indeed," said the Woman. They both laughed. This conversation really made She appreciate her older friend. Sometimes, She felt like she was born in the wrong era. She loved hanging out with someone who enjoyed dressing up as much as she did. They both also appreciated some of the finer things in life, like going to fashion shows, Broadway plays, the symphony and opera, the appreciation of a finely decorated room, and traveling in style. She wished that dancing at a supper club with an orchestra was something she could have experienced. She was envious when her friend would regale her with stories about going out during the war to the nightclubs with officers where there were cigarette girls and the photographers who would go from table to table, taking their pictures, and seeing such stars as Frank Sinatra, Dean Martin, and Lena Horne perform at supper clubs.

She passed on ordering a drink since she'd had her fill on the trip and was trying to cleanse her system now that she was home. Instead, a bartender's ginger ale was her drink of choice. Her older friend raised an eyebrow at her order, but She explained she was not in the mood for alcohol.

She set the soft metallic-looking YSL bag in the vacant chair next to her where it looked like a small child in need of a booster seat. The Birkin was placed across in the other vacant chair where it sat upright like a regal queen. The YSL was one of She's favorites; however, it was starting to show its wear and tear from being used so often. She liked the easy access with the zipper across the top and down a portion of the side, along with the two easy short handles and the simplicity of the bag with the Y formation on each side.

They ordered dinner and settled into the nice conversation rhythm they had developed since their friendship began. She's older friend was always one to have a great story to share.

"Did I ever tell you about my husband's sister?"

"No, do tell," She replied.

"Well, her first husband died in a plane crash, the second died from pneumonia, and the third was killed in a car accident."

"That's terrible," She said.

"I know. She was the kiss of death."

"Did she ever have children?"

"No, she finally settled for a life in her mansion and surrounded herself with a group of lovely gay men who adored her until she died."

"Sounds like an interesting life," said She.

"Yes, she was fun to be around at cocktail parties, and she was always dressed to the nines. For some reason at home, she loved wearing a turban, and it always reminded me of Elizabeth Taylor wandering around her spacious house in her caftans and turban with accents of amazing jewelry."

"Wish I could have been there," said She.

"Me too; you would have loved it. Oh, the parties she would throw. It was like being in a Rita Hayworth movie."

"Stop it; you are making me jealous. How fabulous to be a part of that time in history. I think your generation had all the fun and glamour. Now it seems like those moments are few and far between. Everyone is so casual now, and being crude seems to be the new personality trait."

"Or the next generation is being raised with no manners. I have a niece I love dearly, and her husband is pleasant, but their two teenage girls are a nightmare. When they come to my country estate, they are such inconsiderate little urchins. And the one girl is just a downright bitch. Does not say hello when she arrives or thank you for anything and is sullen most of the time. She makes a mess wherever she goes. It's like that little character on Charlie Brown, you know the one—Pig Pen. Beautiful girl, but I must say she has no sense of class or manners. What she really needs is a semester of lovely lessons. I would be happy to pay for them if it would help. God help my niece. They visited me last month, and upon departing, my niece mentioned they would be coming back next month, so I had to lie and say the week was already booked when it wasn't. Then I had to make arrangements for other friends to come up that weekend just to avoid spending that time with them. Oh, dear, maybe I need lovely lessons."

"Oh, that's awful," said She. "I don't blame you, but it must be hard if you enjoy your niece."

"Yes, but I will be glad when the girls leave for college and start lives of their own," said the Woman and then changed the subject. "How was the trip to Paris with your girlfriends?"

"Oh, it was amazing. We had such a good time, and you know, for spending that much time together, we really traveled well. The previous trip we took to Mexico was right before my first breast cancer surgery."

"Really? You didn't tell me you had cancer. Are you okay?"

"Oh, yes, everything is fine." She proceeded to tell her friend the more positive and humorous version of her diagnosis, surgeries, and recovery.

They continued their lively conversation, and toward the end of their meal, She looked around the beautiful restaurant and said, "You know, this reminds me of the restaurant my aunt used to take me and my cousins to when we were little. It was so fun because we would dress up and all be seated around the elegant round table like adults, and I'll never forget the first time we went with her. We were all seated and being a little noisy, like most small children, and then we got really quiet when she reached into her handbag and drew out a wooden spoon and placed it on the table. We all stared at it, and we knew that if any of us got out of line, she was not opposed to giving us a smack."

"That is so precious," her friend said. "Ah, the universal wooden spoon of the discipline family."

"I know you would not see that today. Now people let their small children run amok. Because God forbid that we stifle their creativity," She said sarcastically.

They had a good laugh and finished their coffee and called it a night. After the bill was settled, they wandered through the hotel lobby, taking in the beauty of their surroundings. The walls were covered in subtle vintage wallpaper and aged wood that seemed to exude the beauty of a bygone era, along with intricate crown moldings, marble floors, heavy draperies, and elaborate floral arrangements. It was the kind of opulence that one can take for granted until you stop to sit in the room and really absorb all that it entails. The fine craftsmanship that went into the design to start with, and then the actual construction and production of all the furniture, lighting, artwork, and accessories, could otherwise go unnoticed. How many times had people rushed through entries, lobbies, restaurants, and meeting places without paying any attention to the warmth and comfort they bring to our everyday lives and the part they play? Our surroundings can be key to some of our behaviors.

They walked through the luxurious lobby after dinner and were quiet until they reached the exterior where She's friend's driver was waiting and offered She a ride, but She decided to walk the few blocks to her apartment since the evening felt so warm and the exercise after a big meal was a good idea.

The walk gave her time to think about her next steps and the good consulting job she was offered, and at that moment, She realized she needed to take the risk and accept the assignment. It would be good to build up her confidence and rely on her instincts that she could handle the three-month assignment. The work would be a welcome distraction from her bouts of depression since quitting her job and give her a purpose every day. The trip had been welcomed and definitely needed for her psyche, and this job also would be good for her self-esteem. This thought made her smile, and she was already planning her next steps and, of course, what to wear!

The company she was consulting for was located in a nice high-rise building not far from her apartment, so the short commute was another plus. The morning her job started, She donned her favorite Dolce & Gabbana suit with matching sheer floral blouse. She selected her Manola Blahnik black pumps and her Lorna Rae bag. She approached the reception desk to announce herself and waited in the tastefully decorated lobby for the VP she had met with the week earlier. When he approached, she couldn't help but feel a little rush of a crush. He was tall, handsome, and had that distinguished calm look about him that made her feel she could trust him with all her savings accounts. He was tall, slender, and his hair was white, but his face was that of a boy. She could just picture him at ten years old in his little league outfit. Even when he smiled, he had that mischievous look about him that made you wonder whether he had just put a frog in your lunchbox and was waiting for you to find it.

They met in the conference room and reviewed the assignment again, and She toured the office to get the layout before she was passed off to a colleague who showed her the office she would call home for a few months. The day flew by as She got a quick tour of the breakroom, restroom location, and how to operate the copy machine. The IT department came by just in time to set up her temporary password and access to the files she would be working on. She spent the rest of the afternoon reading and organizing her project. Next thing she knew, it was way past five o'clock and most of the office had cleared out. She picked up her new temporary access badge and made her way to the elevator to head home. It felt so rewarding to be back at work feeling like she had a purpose. On the way out, she ran into the handsome VP and they exchanged pleasantries about how their day had gone and said goodnight.

She went straight home and texted her best friend to let her know how it was going, but She turned down an invitation to go out. She was tired and wanted to take a warm bath, slip into a comfy nightgown, and get to bed early. She also put together a small bag of personal items to take to the office, such as photos and books, and she wanted to pick up an orchid on the way to work the next day. She needed to surround herself with these items to create a warm work environment.

## | LORNA RAE |

Lorna Rae was sitting near the bench when She returned her to the closet. As usual, the other handbags were all curious about the day and the new job She had accepted.

"There is not much to report," Lorna Rae said, "but the office was nice and She seemed really happy to be there."

That made them all sigh, and they felt like they could all take the first clear breath in months. The tension and worry about being displaced had been lifted.

## | SHE |

She hadn't noticed him at first when they had met months earlier at a fundraiser and sat at the same table. He had that married comfortable look about him, and since She had not dated for years, the thought of looking for someone was not on her mind, so it did not occur to her that he was available or interested.

It was several weeks later when she received an invitation for lunch, and it still never dawned on her that the invitation was anything more than a colleague wanting to discuss a project or a form of networking. Midway through the lunch, it finally occurred to her that he was flirting. It took her by surprise. On the inside her little inner voice was going, *Uh-oh*.

Now it was the third time they had gone out. They had finished a lovely dinner, and he was walking her home. They were approaching her building, and she was getting ready to search through her handbag for her keys. They were almost to the door when he reached out and took her hand and pulled her toward him. The move made her twirl around and land in an embrace and an immediate kiss. The shock and excitement of the moment raced through her, and her Lorna Rae handbag slipped from her hand and fell to the ground, and as She pulled away, she whispered, "Now look what you did."

Lorna Rae could not tell whether the comment was for the dropped handbag or the kiss.

He responded by moving in close to her face, touching forehead to forehead, and saying, "What can I say? I'm a bad man."

*What do we do now?* She thought. It made her nervous, and to make it worse, she was so attracted to this man. Plus, she had not had a relationship in years and was resigned to the fact that being single would be her way of life. She didn't want that to be disrupted, or did She?

She had been through so much stress and conflict the past few years, and now the thought of falling in love and experiencing the happiness she dreamed of since she was young was staring back at her. All of these thoughts ran through her mind at a lightning speed. He must have seen the conflict in her eyes, and perhaps fearful of losing her, he pulled her close in an embrace. He stroked her hair with his hand, and he was so close to her she could feel his breath on her head and his heart was racing.

They stood there in the alcove of her apartment building, sheltered from the pedestrian traffic and any onlookers for a long time, neither one of them wanting to break the spell of the moment.

Finally, She pulled back, and with a smile on her face, she playfully touched his nose and confessed, "I like you."

"I like you too," he said.

They knew the moment's significance and felt secure in pulling away from each other to think about the next steps.

She bent down and retrieved the handbag that fortunately had landed upright on the entry carpet.

It made her like him even more; in the past, the men in her life would have pushed themselves upon her in a selfish way, only thinking of their own needs.

He was different; there was the gentleman side to him, and the fun playful boyish side. He was strong, and at the same time, optimistic and caring.

She entered the apartment and made her way to the closet. Instead of changing right away, she sat on the bench and gazed at the clothes, trying to figure out what to wear to work the next day. She sat there for longer than she should have, but she could not seem to get herself motivated to make any decisions.

The evening's events were so fresh and delicious in her mind, and all she could do was think about the kiss. She reached up and touched her lips and smiled. Wow, when was the last time she had been kissed? She kept reliving the moment in her mind and almost wished the evening had not ended there. *Okay, new thought.*

She selected a fun outfit for the next day, some Akris straight leg pants and jacket, a Lanvin blouse, and the playful Manola Blahnik heels with the mink pompoms. After changing into a slinky silk nightgown, She slipped off to bed.

## | CLOSET |

Lorna Rae was still sitting at the end of the bench where She had left her. The handbag was still touched by the evening's events that she had witnessed, and a little sore from the fall. She had checked the bottom of the bag to make sure there wasn't any damage and just lightly brushed it off with her hand. Normally the neatness in her would have triggered her to wipe down the bag completely, but tonight, it was obvious she was distracted, so she didn't pay much attention to the little mishap earlier.

In all the years Lorna Rae had been with She, there was never a man involved in her life like this, and he was so fun and kind to her that it almost made her a little jealous. Lorna Rae wasn't sure whether she should share the evening with the rest of the bags or hold onto the experience and let it remain a private moment. If the relationship continued, the others would find out soon enough.

The Prada spoke up first, "Hey, where did you go tonight?"

"Just out to dinner."

"Was it with the girls?"

Lorna Rae paused and didn't want to lie, but she still felt prone to keep the night a secret. "It was just a work thing," she finally said. That seemed to do the trick; nobody was that interested to ask more since there was never any reason to think that dinner with a colleague would be different from any other event.

## | SHE |

That Saturday, She's best friend came by to have coffee and they made their way back to the closet so She could loan her friend some jewelry for an event. While in the closet, She confessed to her friend about the recent dating experience.

"Hey, I've been meaning to tell you, but I think I went on a date last week."

"Whaaattttt!" her friend exclaimed. "You, you went on a date...the girl who hasn't been out with a man in how long? As long as I've known you anyway? You just drop it out like that?"

"How else should I have said it?"

"I don't know. I am just a little shocked that you didn't say anything earlier."

"I know it was strange because normally when I sense someone is interested, and especially if we used to work together, I avoid those situations entirely."

"Okay, stop; you are killing me. You worked together? The one man pool you said you would never dip your foot in and never have."

"I know. Stop it; you are not making this any easier. Now you know why it took me so long to tell you."

"Okay, sorry. Please continue because the suspense is killing me."

"He's a nice guy."

"That's a plus since the last one was not."

"I know, and that's why I have stayed away from this for so long. And I have to admit, I'm excited but a little scared. I feel like I am falling into the same patterns as before."

"How so?"

"You know, wondering how much he likes me and how much do I like him?"

"How did this happen?"

"Well, it didn't seem like anything unusual at first because I thought he was just being nice, you know, just meeting to talk about networking and job opportunities. And then midway through, I felt like he was flirting with me, and I was a little taken aback, but at the same time, I didn't hate it."

"Like the times before?"

"Exactly."

"There have been a few other opportunities over the past few years, but I was never interested. Or I would be curious but they weren't. Timing is everything."

"So this time it's different?"

"Yes, because he is so nice to me and we have such a fun time together. And he always seems to know what I'm thinking, which drives me crazy. But it's too soon to tell if anything will come of it."

"This is huge!"

"I know. Now which earrings do you prefer for your event?"

She pulled open one of the drawers that housed her more formal costume jewelry.

"Okay, but don't think we are done discussing this," said She's best friend. "I want to hear everything; I mean details."

"You know I don't kiss and tell."

"He kissed you!"

"Quit acting like I'm fourteen and this is my first date."

"Well, it could be."

"Very funny. Just because I have been out of the dating scene doesn't mean I've forgotten how to do it."

"Have you?"

They both laughed at that one.

"Okay, now I am going to change the subject."

"No you're not."

"You are impossible; you're supposed to be my friend and be completely supportive."

"I am. I support you telling me all the juicy details so I can live vicariously through you."

"It was just, well, really nice, and I don't want to talk about it in detail."

"This *is* someone special if you feel like being so private about it."

"Yeah, and I don't want to jinx it. Who knows? It could be over by next week."

"How optimistic."

"What can I say? I am a cynic at heart."

## Chapter Five

# B = BETRAYAL

**Bette Davis:** *Nice speech, Eve, but I wouldn't worry too much about your heart. You can always put that award where your heart ought to be.*
— All About Eve

She was sitting in her new office when she saw a company email announcing the breast cancer fundraiser lunch invitation, and it made her heart skip a beat. She had not thought about her health experience with breast cancer for some time. All of a sudden, she moved away from the computer and turned her chair to gaze out the window and reflect. Without realizing it, she went from flicking her pen between her fingers to chewing lightly on the end of it. It was around lunchtime and most of the office had stepped out.

Her mind wandered to the diagnosis and all the appointments and procedures that had followed. What had it been now? Three years? That's about right. What a strange time in her life from the mammogram that showed the first few tiny dots clustered on the screen to the full mastectomy and reconstructive surgeries.

It had started in the usual way—having her annual mammogram and then having to go back for a recheck, which was still not alarming, but it was when she had to wait in the small office outside the exam rooms for the doctor that she became concerned. The doctor was a younger man, almost handsome; however, he delivered the news that She should see a surgeon and gave her the recommendation of two in the hospital, like he was recommending a nice place to have lunch. Not much feeling or empathy was included in the bombshell he had just delivered. He must have given that news several times a day until it had taken on little meaning.

She couldn't believe it. All she could think of was what she wanted to say to him, but she had sat in silence. In her head, she wanted to argue, "No, you don't understand; I have smaller boobies; there isn't a lump. I don't smoke, I eat healthy and take care of myself, and this doesn't run in my family." There was no reason this situation should be happening. She was reeling and in denial and spent the next six months doing research before seeing another doctor and going through the painful needle biopsy that delivered the unfortunate news, breast cancer.

After researching, She declined the radiation therapy and opted for a double mastectomy and reconstructive surgery. She didn't want to have to think about a possible reoccurrence, and if the cancer came back, it would probably be difficult to do the reconstructive surgery after radiation. Her life became a time of decisions and planning; selecting a surgeon, a plastic surgeon, and finding an oncologist, and eventually, scheduling the three surgeries. She had already been through two biopsies and was ready to get this behind her.

She thought about the wonderful trip to Mexico prior to the first surgery—a double mastectomy. She had traveled with three of her best friends to a luxury resort and spent the week hanging out at a gorgeous house on the beach. They would get up each morning and make breakfast and eat it at the dining table located on the patio. Trips to town were made to pick up a few supplies, and they even located a Starbucks to get their coffee. They played a little tennis and golf, but they spent most of their time at the pool at the house, reading and listening to music, and in the evenings, watching movies. She smiled when she remembered how they would whisper the word "cancer" to make light of it as a coping mechanism. Of course, She started it. "I'm sorry; I can't do that—I have cancer," she would say and laugh.

One afternoon, they were all singing on the patio by the pool to all of the greatest hits from the '70s, and since the pool faced the beach, they noticed the paparazzi (aka/ fishing) boat go back and forth in the ocean; however, it was funny because the photos would not reveal the celebrities they were hoping to capture—they were just four regular girls having a good time.

Her mind wandered back to the diagnosis, and She remembered that strange feeling when you realize your body has betrayed you and not knowing how this happened or why, and wondering whether it will come back. It's weird when you can't control what's going on inside of you.

Being an organized person, She made arrangements for good friends to stay with her during each surgery; the first was the mastectomy, and a month later, the expander surgery was done, and then came the final surgery three months later to add the implants.

She smiled when she thought of how interesting it had been going to the plastic surgeon's office during that time to fill the expanders. Every one or two weeks, they would add another 50cc's of saline to each breast, and the breasts would expand like in a cartoon. *Keep that sense of humor*, She thought. *It's critical.*

She was so grateful to have such wonderful, compassionate friends there to take care of her. Even though they had to travel to get there, she sent them plane tickets and had local friends pick them up at the airport. It seemed better to have her out-of-town friends assist since it gave her a chance to see them, and it gave her local friends a break from all the appointments they had helped with to date.

However, all the organizing in the world did not prepare her for some of the surprises during her recovery; not being able to use her arms after the expander surgery for two days made it impossible to get in and out of bed without assistance, and she developed a fever a few times and the pain killers had made her sick.

## | LORNA RAE |

Lorna Rae had sat in the chair next to She in the surgeon's office while She went over the mammograms, test results, and options with the doctor. There were not very many tears; She was only devoting energy to choosing a path and planning the double mastectomy and reconstructive surgeries, three in all.

The closet had been especially quiet that day since the handbags knew something had happened by the phone call from the doctor and the tears. There had been several trips to the doctor and a couple of biopsies and the result was cancer. Panic escalated to an all-time high after the first major surgery, and they had all feared the worst. What if something happened to She and they were all displaced? Where would they end up? Change was always frightening, but having them all leave the closet at the same time was really scary. The month She was home recovering was odd because none of the bags left the closet, and She only donned her silk pants and button-up top pajamas every day.

"I can't believe this is happening!" the handbags said to one another. "What are we going to do this time?"

"This is serious; did you see how skinny she has become and how scary the surgery scars are?"

"And those drains she had to deal with coming out of her chest and pinned to her pajamas. How did she sleep?"

"Not well, didn't you notice how she gets up almost every night and is watching TV?"

"The first few days were tough when she would get ill, I know, because I heard her. She yelled at her friend not to come in the bathroom, and she hugged the toilet and spilled her breakfast after the pain pills reacted negatively."

"We haven't gone out for a month, and who knows when we will go out again?"

"Don't be so negative. She looks better today, and she's been doing her hair and makeup even though she still has to live in her p.j.'s and is not able to go out."

"The fact that she is in pretty good spirits is encouraging and that she has her friends taking good care of her."

"Yeah, you may be right, but we have all been cooped up in here for weeks. I'm tired of sitting on this shelf; my dust cover is chafing me."

"Very funny; you can't chafe from a soft flannel cover wrapped around you. She is going to be fine, and we will get to go out before you know it."

"What if we don't?"

"Well, let's worry about that when the time comes. It doesn't do us any good to turn on each other and become more paranoid than we already are."

"I am so tired of your Pollyanna style and wish you would just let the rest of us vent."

"Okay fine; go at it, you worn-out has-been."

"What does that mean? She still takes me out."

"Yeah, but you are only a style away from being consigned, or better yet, donated."

"That's just cruel; what makes you so special? At least I have a classic style that is still desired."

"By whom? Old ladies and queens?"

"You better mean the type of queen who rules a country."

"Sure."

The next thing you knew, Chanel pulled at City's tassel and City used her handle to take a swing at her attacker's pocket with a punch.

"All right, that's enough," said Lorna Rae. "She is very sick, and we don't need to be taking out our anger over the situation on each other."

The closet got quiet and nobody spoke for the rest of the evening. The quiet of the closet was becoming a norm and nobody liked it. They missed She coming into the closet and putting together a fun outfit, choosing a handbag, and going about her day. Sometimes when She purchased a new piece, She would come home and try it on with several outfits like she was doing a little mini-fashion show. Even though the bags would laugh about some of her selections later, they missed the silly ritual. Given the current situation, it almost made them feel guilty about making fun of her. They would give anything now to witness a home-style runway show.

## | SHE |

She's thoughts about her breast cancer experience were interrupted when her cell phone vibrated and She noticed her best friend was calling.

"Hey, how are you, and how is the new temp job?" She's friend asked.

"It's great. I'm just sitting here looking out the window, deep in thought."

"They pay you to do that?"

"Very funny. I just saw an invitation to a Breast Cancer fundraiser and it brought back a few memories."

"Oh, I'm sorry. I didn't mean to sound so flip."

"No worries. I was just thinking about our trip to Mexico and how much fun it was."

"Thanks again for making those arrangements."

"My pleasure, my friend; hey, how about meeting after work?"

"Sure."

"Hey, by the way, how is Mr. Dreamy?"

"Cute. He is good, but he's been traveling this week, so all we have done is sent a few personal texts to each other. He gets back at the end of the week."

"I still think you should pursue this one."

"I know; let's talk more about this tonight. I don't want to discuss it while I'm on the J-O-B."

"Okay, Secret Agent Lovebird."

"Very funny. See you at the same bat time and same bat channel."

"You got it."

After She ended the call, she started to think about how complicated relationships seem to get as we get older, and yet at the same time, you don't tolerate the things you didn't like from earlier dating years. Take sex, for example; in your early dating experience, you would try anything and it seemed there was always a lover who wanted to bend you like a pretzel into some Kama Sutra position that was so distracting it was like trying to play Twister in bed. Not only did you lose your orgasm, but your dignity, too.

## | LORNA RAE |

Lorna Rae was sitting on the windowsill of the new office that She had been occupying the past few weeks. It felt good to be back at work with She and watching her do what she loved. The office was gorgeous and had a fun and professional atmosphere, so Lorna Rae had been happy to join She almost every day the past week. She would set her on the credenza or counter by the window of the high-rise where Lorna Rae had a fantastic view of the city skyline. At She's past job, Lorna Rae was usually stowed away for safekeeping in one of her large desk drawers. For some reason, this office was so elegant and relaxed that Lorna Rae spent most of her time out in the open on display. She was in her office most of the time and only stepped out for the occasional meeting, at which point, Lorna Rae was stowed beneath the desk.

As the deadline approached for her consulting job to come to an end, Lorna Rae sensed that She was sad at the idea of leaving the company and office she had grown to find challenging and fulfilling. It was then She decided to request a meeting with the VP to discuss any chance of continuing on as a full-time employee. What did she have to lose? The project she was working on was finished ahead of schedule, and they had found another for her to take over until her contract period ran out.

As it happened, She received an email the following day to meet with the VP, and before she could request the extension, he started asking her questions that led to the final one of "How would you like to stay on full-time as a permanent hire?" Lorna Rae was very pleased by this turn of events. The Handbag liked the elegant office and having a break from being in the closet with the sometimes too nosey handbags.

# | SHE |

Mr. Dreamy called She later that afternoon and they decided to meet for a drink. They went to her favorite bar and settled into a flirty conversation. It was obvious they liked each other and had an easy way of teasing each other. She loved the way he looked at her, and he seemed to like everything about her. She thought he was so sexy—just looking at him made her twinge.

At one point, She was telling him a story and stopped.

"You aren't even listening to me are you?"

He grinned.

"I'll bet you've already started to undress me and are making your way south."

He laughed and reached under the table to touch her knee.

They continued the conversation, but he seemed to be distracted and nervous at the same time. She sensed he had something to say, but he was afraid to tell her.

During his second drink, and with much obvious hesitation, he dropped a bomb she was not expecting.

"I want you to know, and I need to tell you because I respect you." He paused, shook his head, and took another drink. "I have a girlfriend, a longtime girlfriend, and we live together."

She could not believe what she was hearing; that was the last thing she had expected. When he had said he had something to tell her and looked pained, She didn't know what to think—certainly, she had not expected anything that would impact her so strongly. They had not known each other that long, and in her mind, it was obvious this relationship was now over.

It was devastating. She had to sit there and nod her head and act understanding. He told her how much he liked and admired her, and how pretty and smart she was. All she could think to ask was, "Why didn't you tell me during the first time we had lunch?"

He said he didn't expect to have such a good time, and he had liked what he saw, which made him want more.

She wanted to believe him, but at the same time, she felt like a fool. Why did she let herself fall for this guy? It was not like her. Was her radar so off that this one incident confirmed she really had no business dating or even attempting a relationship? Are all men, as Holly Golightly had stated, rats or super rats?

What She dreamed as a girl and now dared to dream as a grown woman was "poof" gone. It was like an evil queen had struck her with a jeweled orb and then laughed at her foolishness.

There was that princess theory again of finding the man of your dreams. She was worried that as more time went by, there would be no more time.

It made her wonder whether moving forward she would have to create a laundry list of screening questions before she went out with anyone. Of course, there were the obvious ones of "Are you married? Do you have a girlfriend? Are you separated? And then there were the more particular ones that don't always have relevance when it comes to love, but beg the question. Do you have a job? Have you ever been arrested? Are you an alcoholic or drug addict? Do you have an extensive porn collection? How many ex-wives do you have? Any juvenile delinquent children?" The list could go on, but what a mood killer and She didn't want to look at love that way.

It was as if the last few years of taking time off from dating to heal and find out what had gone wrong with the other men she had dated, to make sure she didn't repeat this pattern, was no help at all. The dating gods were laughing their asses off to think she could be so foolish as to outsmart them.

The evening had to end. He kept on talking, and She knew it was his way of not wanting to walk away, but at this point, she had stopped listening.

She finally said, "We need to go." She couldn't take any more of this. All She wanted to do was run away.

She could only think about putting one foot in front of the other as they left the restaurant. For some reason, She was focused on the light changing so they could cross the street. Everything was in slow motion, and her life had just changed as quickly as the light.

He walked her to her door, but instead of a lovely kiss, it was awkward, and she tried to joke it away by sticking out her hand to say goodbye with a handshake and then hugging him.

All she could say was "See you around," and that was it. Checkmate. Game over. Crap.

She knew he cared for her, and she was crazy about him, so she wanted to get to know him more. He had stirred something in her that no man ever had; she ached for him. It was like all those really bad romance novels she had read when she was a teenager, and now, at this point in her life, when she saw them on the grocery store shelf, they made her roll her eyes in exasperation. She would think to herself, *That stuff never happens in real life*. And now look where she was, sliding off the pages of some tattered paperback.

Another night of crawling in the tub and having a good cry. Ugh. She was back here again, an emotional place she had avoided for years. When would She find a man who did not make her cry? But this time was different. She felt pissed and a little destructive. She wanted a drink, and then another drink, and then a cigarette. She left the apartment and headed down her street, walking several blocks until She found a sleepy bar that for some reason still allowed smoking inside. Thank God.

She didn't have any fear about her safety at that moment. There was a scrappy aura around her that said, "Don't even think about it," and on the flip side, her attitude of "I don't care" was apparent from her walking for thirty minutes in one of her favorite pair of Manolo heels.

She sat alone at one end of the bar and ordered a whiskey. She felt like Greta Garbo and wanted to add, "And don't be stingy, baby," but she decided against it. This guy wouldn't get the premise.

The warmth and sting of the hard alcohol were soothing. She could feel the liquor glide down her throat and mingle throughout her body, and the warm tingle spread through her bloodstream, reaching every point. The lovely buzz kicked in and she felt relaxed. It gave her a chance to reflect and try to get some perspective. She was thinking how most people would go to their therapist to talk such situations out, but this was her therapy of choice. No talking, just drinking and thinking. She wanted to solve this situation on her own, if there were a solution; more like figure out a way to get it out of her system. And the drinks were doing the trick.

Her mind started to wander and she thought about how charming he had been; he had a Ph.D. in flirting and flattery; in fact, he could teach. She pictured him as Foghorn Leghorn in a cartoon, talking to the youngster he was always trying to coach. "Now see here, boy; listen up. The key to a woman's heart is to tell her what she wants to hear—flattery, boy. Are you listening? Compliment her hair, tell her how pretty and smart she is. Did you get all that, boy? Now where did he go? Won't have any more chicks in the barn if the boy can't learn how to land a woman."

She was definitely now a little drunk and amused by her thoughts. She wished this little bit of heavenly state could last longer. Maybe this was why some people drink continually. Was there that much pain in the world? Too bad she couldn't hold her liquor. "Lightweight," she mumbled. This was really not a classy side of herself, but right now, she enjoyed it, and who would find out anyway? That was one advantage to being on your own— you are not beholden to anyone for taking small detours from your life.

She bummed a cigarette from the bartender and he lit it for her.

"Hey, haven't seen you in here before?" he flirted. "What brings you in tonight?"

She just looked at him with an icy stare. He, like most young bartenders, was gorgeous and obviously had no trouble finding women.

"What's a nice girl like you doing out on a night like this all alone?" he persisted.

A long pause. "Tough day?"

No response. "Must be man troubles."

She was annoyed.

"Okay, I can see you are just trying to drown your sorrows."

"No, I'm just teaching them how to dog-paddle," she said sarcastically.

He chuckled at her reply and leaned in to make another comment, but She gave him that look that said, "We are done talking now," while taking a long drag on the cigarette. He pulled his hands back in a "Don't shoot me" pose and said, "Okay, you win." He wandered back to the other side of the bar to chat with a few men who were drinking and watching the news on the TV overhead.

Her mind began to wander again, and this time, the thoughts were deeper. What did she want and expect from her life? What is it about passion that can be so exciting and satisfying, and the next thing you know, you are in an opposite polar with regret and humiliation? But this situation was not like the others. He really wasn't a bad man. He just didn't come clean about his situation until it was too late for her in regards to her emotional investment. Maybe what she really liked the most was how he made her feel. Maybe she was enamored with how he saw her. Was that the major attraction? She knew that wasn't true, but somehow the rationale, made her feel better, and it relieved some of the shame she felt at the moment. The life they could have had together made her feel so sad that suddenly two tears escaped and slid down her cheek.

The next emotion triggered her to think about how troubling it was that a guy who had a nice woman at home would even be out looking at another woman. Was she better off not having this work out? Would she find herself in this same position in a few years when he would tire of her and be out flirting with someone else? When did these grown-up problems become so complicated?

After finishing her second drink and stubbing out the smoldering and barely smoked cigarette, She pulled out her cell phone and called a cab. In her state, it was not wise to walk back home. She placed some money on the bar to cover the drinks and a handsome tip to adjust for the free cigarette and appreciation of being left alone. When the cab arrived, She slid off her barstool, grabbed Lorna Rae, and headed home.

When she reached home, She dropped the handbag in the closet on the bench, left her clothes in a pile on the floor, and just slipped into a T-shirt and headed straight to bed. She didn't even wash her face or brush her teeth. "What's the point and who cares?" was the attitude of the evening.

In the morning when she was taking some aspirin and preparing coffee, She reflected on the night before and somehow found it amusing, even though her head and stomach did not. *It's interesting how as you get older, the heartaches are easier to get over*, she thought, *or is that wishful thinking?*

Her cell phone was ringing and she realized it was still in her handbag in the closet. Making her way to the back of the apartment, she opened the closet door and saw the state of her mind from the night before. The bag was lying on its side with some of its contents spilled out, and her clothes were in a pile on the floor.

*Oh dear, this is a bit of a mess*, she thought. She found the phone, and upon saying, "Hello," her words were groggy since it was the first time she had spoken that day and the hangover made her voice scratchy.

"Good morning. Oh, did I wake you?" It was She's best friend.

"No, I was awake."

"Are you sure?"

"*Yes*, I have been up for about half an hour." She was actually a little amused at this questioning and asked her friend, "Why is it when you ask someone if they were sleeping when you call, they always say, 'No'? It's the universal response."

Her friend responded, "I know. I think it's because they are either embarrassed to be sleeping at that hour, or they don't want to make you feel bad you woke them up."

"Or both," said She.

They laughed.

"What are you doing?" asked her friend.

"Nursing a hangover."

"What? What did you do?"

"You don't want to know."

"Are you alone?"

"Of course I am; that's my story, always alone."

"Uh oh, what went wrong with the new romance?"

"The worst; let me call you back later; I need aspirin and coffee."

# | CLOSET |

In the closet that evening, the bags turned to Lorna Rae and were asking about what had happened that night.

"What is going on?" Prada asked. "She is clearly drunk and smells like an ashtray."

Lorna Rae was upset too, but she didn't know how to tell them since she had kept the new romance a secret, and it had not come out to the rest of them because it ended so quickly. Plus, she was horrified at where She and she had gone that night.

"Well, She was seeing this man," Lorna Rae finally said.

"Whhhaattt?" said the Balenciaga. "According to the gossip in this closet, She has not had a man around since we have all been here, except for Beady, who met the last one, and we all know from her that was painful."

"Anyway," continued Lorna Rae, "as you can imagine, it did not last long, and She is pretty upset."

"What happened?" chimed in the Lanvin Pop clutch.

"Apparently, he has a girlfriend."

"Well, if he had a girlfriend, why did he invite her out?" asked the Fendi naively.

"I don't know how men think," said Lorna Rae. "I guess he liked her and wanted to get to know her. But he didn't anticipate liking her so much and so quickly and then had to come clean."

"Maybe he needs to be smacked on the nose with a rolled up newspaper like the bad dog he is," said the Prada.

"Wow, and you were there to witness the whole thing?" said the Chanel tote.

"Yes, I was sitting on the chair and witnessed the entire train wreck."

"How did she respond when she heard the news?" asked the Prada.

"Oh, you know; she was trying to be understanding and make light of it, but I could tell a few times her eyes were getting misty."

"Wow, you get to see all the exciting stuff," said YSL inappropriately.

"This is one conversation I wish I had missed," replied Lorna Rae. "But it didn't end there. After he dropped her off, She ended up going to this horrible smelly little bar and proceeded to drink and smoke. I have never seen her like that. Ugh, I smell terrible, and I think I sat in something sticky."

"Oh, you will air out. But I wish she had left you on the patio; you are starting to smell up the place along with the pile of couture on the floor," said the Balenciaga.

"I wouldn't worry too much about it," said Beady.

They all turned to her in surprise because Beady usually never said much. But having seen this type of behavior in her original owner's previous life, Beady knew it would pass and told the rest of the group the same. "She just needed to blow off a little steam. If I know a strong woman, she will be fine."

As is typical when something unnerving happens, the handbags retreated to their dust covers and called it a night.

"I hope She is okay," the Pochette added.

### | SHE |

A few weeks later, after putting her night of drunken therapy behind her, She decided to have a nice quiet celebration of her new job with a few of her team members at the restaurant in the office building's lobby. They all gathered there in the bar.

They had a great time and left the restaurant early since most of She's colleagues had families to get home to. She met up with a couple of her girlfriends to continue the celebration at a new restaurant near her apartment that was sure to be a hot spot that evening.

They had only been there a few minutes and had just ordered drinks. They were distracted by the number of people in the restaurant and were getting up and making their way around the table to say hello to each other.

It happened so quickly—like a thief, because it was a thief. She turned around and panic rushed through her whole body. The Lorna Rae was gone!

She immediately pushed the chair aside to look under the table and then scanned the crowded restaurant. It was as if everything just stopped, and when looking back, those following moments were a blur for her. She turned to her dinner companions and asked whether they had seen her handbag. The look of panic on her face immediately crossed everyone else's face, and they all looked to see whether their handbags were safe. She stopped the waitress passing by and asked for the manager. She told him her bag was gone, and then she ran out the front door to see whether she could find the perpetrator. She wanted to scream and cry all at the same time, and her hands were clenched in fists at her side. The anger and fear consumed her. She ran back into the restaurant and asked a friend to call the police. Everything she had in that bag was gone; everything that was important at that moment—her wallet, keys, calendar, checkbook; what else was missing from her life that would be difficult and painful to replace? She knew she had to get home quickly to her safe to get the credit card information and call to cancel her cards. But she had to wait for the police to show up and find out whether anybody at the restaurant had seen anything. The only thing anyone saw was a well-dressed couple drift through like they were looking for someone and immediately go out again. Nobody noticed the handbag. How could they not notice the Lorna Rae? She felt flushed—her favorite bag was gone and even though the contents were important, it was the bag that meant the most to her. The only good point was her cell phone was in her hand at the moment because she had taken a moment to check her messages right before the bag was snatched.

While She was waiting for the police, she called her building manager to get her a copy of her apartment key. She searched through her phone and called her two main credit card companies to alert them to the theft and had them help her put a hold on all her accounts. The restaurant was so gracious and gave her a glass of wine and offered her a free dinner, but She was too upset to drink or eat. She waited outside, and when the police arrived, they took her report. Then she left the restaurant and headed home to meet her building manager so she could get back into her home. Such small, everyday gestures were now a stressful event. The thought of having to replace all her cards, get a new driver's license…barf, the DMV waiting in line, having to prove you exist, trying to take a decent picture. But, back to her precious Lorna

Rae—where was she now? What was to become of her, and would she ever see her again?

While talking to the police officer earlier, She had asked this question about the odds of getting her handbag back. He had just sighed and tried to be reassuring. Poor guy, trying to help some silly girl find her missing purse was not going to be a priority in his world, and it shouldn't be. But golly gee…damn.

She knew that in the grand scheme of things, this was not an earth-shattering event, and it would pass, but at the moment, it was difficult and she felt so violated. Why did they single her out? How many times was she so careful about keeping an eye on her purse and being mindful about safety whether in the car or at home? She was always locking doors, wearing a seatbelt, looking both ways when crossing the street, keeping her handbag close and an eye on her luggage when traveling. What had caused her for just a few moments to lose track of that caution and become another statistic?

By the time she got home and got into her safe and made the rest of the necessary phone calls, she was exhausted. All of a sudden, she realized the thief had her address and keys to her apartment. Fear-induced adrenaline kicked in, and she then called a locksmith to come out and change her locks.

The sadness consumed her; it was so many things that had roller-coastered into one; the betrayal of her health, those who had contributed to the end of her job, the romance that had ended, and now the loss of her one prized possession and all that it contained. She felt the months of situations catch up with her, and the sobs rolled out of her like a tiny volcano. It was like a tiny part of her had died. She ended up in the closet, trying to get ready for bed, but she was brought to her knees by the sadness that consumed her. It came on so suddenly that she did not feel it; strength was what she was all about and what others expected from her. But in the silence of her sanctuary, she felt overwhelmed and could not hold back any longer. Seriously, this was not the end of the world, but her security was spinning out of her control, and she needed to figure out how to get it back. But for now, she had to let it out—it needed somewhere to go.

## I CLOSET I

It was obvious from the moment She came home that something was terribly wrong and the handbags' world was about to change. It sent a chill through the closet when they heard She on the phone, ordering a locksmith to change the locks and explaining that her handbag had been stolen. She had to find some cash in her safe to pay the locksmith when he was finished. With all her credit cards in lockdown mode, it was a good thing she kept a little cash on hand.

What the handbags witnessed that evening took their breath away. They had never seen She so upset or express such emotion. When she had dealt with cancer, there had been some tears, but this was something new. When she came into the closet to get ready for bed, they could see she had been crying, but this was indeed a meltdown that gave them pause. She sat on the bench and then crumbled to the floor, sobbing. Some of the handbags could not look at such a sad sight; they felt bad enough knowing that Lorna Rae was gone, but they knew this grief went deeper. The loss of her job and the changes to her body had finally taken their toll. She had every right to break down in the one place she felt the safest—her closet. She was surrounded by the items that brought her such joy; although they tended to seem a bit superficial, in the end, they were what made her feel protected. There are moments in life when we don't need to worry about what others think or whether what we feel is appropriate; we just need to feel in the safety of our own environment.

After She left to go to bed, it was a long time before anyone had the courage to speak up.

"I feel terrible," said the YSL. "We were so hard on Lorna Rae, and now that the matriarch of the closet is gone, I know it will not be the same without her."

The rest of the bags looked at each other, but nobody could say anything more. This was a death in their world. It was one of those moments that made them all realize how important life was, and nobody had the nerve to speak up. Sometimes, it's better not to say anything.

So much sadness in such a little closet.

## | SHE |

She went to bed that night with so many thoughts spinning through her mind. What was happening to so many people these days? What had happened to integrity? She thought about what had happened to her previous job and wondered why so many people think it's okay to hurt you or say they are behind you, but the minute something goes wrong, they throw you under the bus to save themselves? The old movies and novels had shown how the good guy always prevails and the person who did him wrong either gets his karma or feels bad and apologizes, but those days were gone. Why were some people unwilling to admit they had made a mistake and feel bad and want to try to make it right? They always wanted to blame someone else and say, "I didn't know; therefore, I don't have to apologize." What was that? It was like the people who abused Twelve Step programs. They would do something unkind and then try to explain to you that the reaction you were having was your problem.

Such moments must be meant to challenge our own integrity and teach us how to handle such conflicts to build our own characters and give us the ability to forgive and move on with our lives. Because, certainly, the person who did us wrong is not the least bit worried about how he affected us or why he should continue to care.

And now the combination of leaving her former job and the betrayal of her health and the stolen handbag made her angry. She thought the previous challenges were behind her and she was at the end of feeling that way, but the latest crisis brought out this anger and she knew it. Having someone take such a personal item from her in a public place was unacceptable.

But it was a private anger, not the kind She could really share with those around her without being looked upon as a somewhat shallow and selfish person. It was time to pull out the bedroom pillow and throw a few punches.

# Chapter Six

# A = ACCEPTANCE

**Cary Grant:** *How would you like a spanking?*
**Audrey Hepburn:** *How would you like*
*a punch in the nose?*
— Charade

The holidays were always a favorite time of She's, and the cocktail party at her older friend's penthouse was the one event to which she was really looking forward. Selecting the dress was the first order of business, and her Natalie Wood beaded evening handbag was already picked out for the occasion. She chose her sleek TSE spaghetti strap dress with a satin top and cashmere skirt, and for jewelry, a short cluster of pearls necklace accented with a large vintage Weiss rhinestone broach. All of this was topped off with her recent purchase of a sheared mink short jacket, soft as butter, and a pair of Manola Blahnik bejeweled pumps.

She made an appointment with her favorite makeup artist and stopped by the department store in the early afternoon on the day of the event to get her face on. She admired those makeup artists who could wield their brushes in such a way that mere mortals could not.

## | BEADY |

The evening bag was so excited when She picked her from the shelf and gently stroked her hand over the beaded exterior in admiration. It had a small chain handle, and its interior was a well-preserved satin lining with a tiny pocket. Even though many years before the bag had belonged to movie star, Natalie Wood, the life in She's closet was a comfortable retreat for her, and the little vintage bag cherished the few times leaving the closet. The memories of those glamorous New York and Hollywood days were distant, but every now and then, they would come to the little bag in a dream and make her feel grateful for the good life she had experienced.

The bag was purchased in New York at Saks Fifth Avenue, and her exterior was made entirely of gorgeous pale pearl beads, for which she became known as Beady by her closet roommates.

Beady now felt She fill her with a small Chanel wallet, cell phone, lipstick, and tissue. These items were not much different from those of her previous owner except for the cell phone. This new phenomenon still took her by surprise when it would ring or vibrate, yet it was a given for the rest of the handbags in the closet who had experienced the cell phone from their beginnings. She put on long satin gloves and grasped the tiny bag before heading out the door. The house keys were the last item placed in the bag, and then they were off to the party.

Going out was always a series of unpredictable events when you combined festivities, drinking, and the expectation to celebrate late into the night. There seemed to be an agreement among evening bags that what happens on those rare occasions is their own little secret. On the rare times Beady had left the closet, she had always been tight-lipped about what happened, not like a former evening bag who had talked non-stop about the parties and shenanigans witnessed. Beady felt a certain loyalty and discretion due to her origination in a different time—a time when privacy was part of being a Lady.

Beady enjoyed the time early on during the parties when all the evening bags were clustered on the master bedroom bed along with a variety of men's overcoats and women's furs. All of the bags were so interesting, and they had such fun stories to tell. Beady typically did not say much about her history, but if there were another vintage bag there, it was fun to reminisce about past parties and the anticipation of what was in store for the rest of the evening. It was a safe place to talk since they would inevitably not see each other again.

However, Beady could also be extremely private, a lot like her original owner. At this point in her existence, she was happy to be retired in a closet where the current owner appreciated her significance.

This party was no exception to most other cocktail parties where the coats and bags were piled on the bed; however, at this party, one of the guest bedrooms was used and not that of the hostess. The room was tastefully elegant and decorated to be more inviting than most guest bedrooms. The bedding was high quality, and the room had all the personal touches to make one feel at home. Current magazines were on the lower level of the nightstand, and on top was a small candy dish filled with expensive chocolates. Hidden touches included a TV inside the giant armoire, and in the closet was a cozy robe and slippers, along with extra pillows and blankets.

At this point in the evening, several coats were on the bed, including some women's furs and the array of elegant evening bags. One of the other bags on the bed was a fun Judith Leiber bag in the shape of a bear. Another evening bag was covered in rhinestones, and yet another was a Lanvin box-shaped clutch covered in jewels. There were a few other Leiber looking bejeweled bags and what appeared to be a Lulu Guinness bag resembling an elegant flowerpot, a satin Prada clutch in gold, and a vintage Chanel evening bag.

With the party in full swing, the bags seemed to be evenly placed around the bed and staring each other down, wondering who would speak first or whether they would just assume their positions and remain silent throughout the evening. They were so used to being quiet and not going out very often that it did not seem unusual to behave this way.

Beady decided it was now or never and struck up a conversation with the group. Not that she was one to brag, but she knew it would be a good conversation starter to talk a little bit about her former life. At a glance, it was obvious she was a vintage bag and could be written off as something not that special. However, her life experiences typically outshone those of any other bag at a party. Beady introduced herself by sharing the moment she joined Natalie Wood during her honeymoon in New York when she had married Robert Wagner (for the first time; they were married twice). The actress and her actor husband were staying at the Waldorf Towers and she had come into Saks for a quick shopping trip and found the beautiful bag. From the moment her famous owner touched the little bag, it knew it was in for an adventure.

The actress had approached the counter with her husband and a male friend, and when she had peered into the case, she had pointed out the bag. The saleswoman had removed it from the shelf and presented it to the young star. The bag had never seen such a beautiful woman and was mesmerized from the moment she ran her fingers across the beaded exterior; it sent a chill through the bag, who could not believe her luck. It was wrapped and quickly presented to the famous customer, who then rushed toward the elevator to continue her shopping spree. There seemed to be a buzz that followed her wherever she went in public. At first, it baffled the tiny handbag, but as time went on, she came to realize the significance of her original owner.

The time in Manhattan was filled with the Wagners attending Broadway plays and being photographed leaving restaurants. The bag found the evenings out in New York to be an ongoing parade of fun and frolic. The little bag was filled with tiny lipstick stains from those precious evenings that made the interior silk lining look like a child's first attempt with a crayon to paper.

The other handbags were in awe—how fabulous to have witnessed such events. The Lanvin confessed that the closest she had come to any type of celebrity was at a charity event that involved photographs of her and her owner making it to the newspaper fashion section.

The Leiber Bear hopped over and landed on a soft mink, and its eyes seemed to widen at the thought of such a life. "I'm usually placed on the table at an event and get passed around a lot with oohs and aahs, like a baby being admired, and then I end up as the centerpiece at the table," said the Leiber Bear. Leiber bags are an object of painstaking luxury; every Swarovski crystal is applied by hand to the bag, which makes it look like a jewel box.

"But," added the Bear, "you really experienced some fun, didn't you?"

Before Beady could answer, the Bear tipped over onto the mink.

"Oh...this mink is cozy," said the Bear as it fell back and sank into the luxurious fur.

The rest of the bags laughed at the little bear's silly actions.

Beady's celebrity life was short-lived, but she knew that experiencing only a few great events in your life was better than years of an uneventful life. "It was lovely," Beady responded. They all seemed to reflect on the story and about their own limited lives outside their closets.

Beady did not go into the details that led to her years of being stored in the closet and then being passed along to a friend, who eventually sold the bag to the dealer whom She had purchased her from. Beady felt it was best not to focus on those lonely moments and instead to remember how fortunate she was to be at this party in this room, surrounded by what was turning out to be a fun gaggle of evening bags.

Evening bags are special creatures that can have a short shelf-life or one of several years with the same owner. There is usually no rhyme or reason to their fate.

"Okay, what's the best party you have ever been to, or what event is the most memorable?" Beady asked the others.

The Leiber Bear spoke up first. "I've got one and you can repeat it, but I'll change the names to protect the innocent. Well, my owner was dating a much younger man one time, and they had gone to one of these events, and when the driver brought them home, they were quite giddy and a little intoxicated. And by the way, this guy was gorgeous; they started making out in the hallway and through the door and, of course, straight to the bedroom. I was clutched in my owner's hand the whole time until the clothes started coming off, and then I slipped out of her hand and landed on the carpet. Fortunately, I was not hurt and rolled toward one of the chairs in the sitting room of the bedroom. Well, the next thing I know, his boxers were tossed and landed right on top of me and I passed out. The next thing I remember, I was back in the closet in the lighted cabinet."

"That's terrifying!" one of the bags exclaimed.

"I think it's hilarious," another one said.

"Can you believe it—men's shorts landed on my head and poof out like a light," said the Bear.

"Sounds like you were gassed."

"Guess I'm not equipped for stinky shorts."

"I hope she gave you a bath before you were put back in the closet."

"And the worst part," said the Leiber Bear, "is now the rest of my closet friends have dubbed me Pooh Bear."

"Okay, my turn," the Lanvin bejeweled clutch said. "I was at this event a few months ago with my owner, and I could feel her senses heighten; then I knew why. There he was, the man who got away. Her heart leapt inside her chest and was racing; he saw her too and tilted his head and smiled at her. God, he looked great, standing there in his suit with a cocktail in his hand. It had been months since they had seen each other, and he had left her for another woman.

"He strode toward her, and without saying a word, gave her a big hug. You could feel the excitement and electricity of their emotions. I was clutched in her hand, and when she reached around to hug him, I could feel his rapid heart rate and hers to match.

"When they pulled apart, he smiled and said, 'You have been on my mind, and I wanted so many times to pick up the phone and call you.' She just stared back at him with her big, beautiful eyes that he loved.

"They stood there for what seemed like an eternity before they spoke, and then things turned to making the typical small talk of 'How are you? Nice party,' and eventually, he couldn't hold back any longer.

"'I wanted to let you know I am single,' he said.

"There was this large pause, and the anticipation of what would happen next was killing me," said the handbag.

"He added, 'But I needed some time to go by before contacting you, and I wasn't sure if you would want to see me or if you were seeing anyone.'

"You could tell he was so frightened of what her response would be; his eyes moved down to the floor as he finished his sentence.

"Without saying anything, my owner took his hand and they made their way out onto one of the vacant patios. The party inside was in full swing, and for some reason, this veranda was unoccupied. They didn't waste any time on words. She leaned toward him to give him the green light. He pulled her into him and kissed her deeply. You could feel the kiss run all the way through her.

"What happened next didn't really fall under one of the more classy exits from a party—more like a Jerry Lewis comedy sketch. They could not find their coats fast enough to say goodbye to the hostess and get his car from the valet. Anyone at the party who witnessed the scene could see their clothes were going to be peeled off as fast as the car ripped out of the driveway."

The other bags let out a hoot. It was one of those nights where the fun of hanging out on the bed and being away from their closets and among their own kind made it even more fun to dish. Normally, they were taken to such formal events that they had no possibility of being able to socialize with other bags. With everyone on the bed, it was like a big slumber party playing truth or dare.

Even the gorgeous vintage Chanel bag was laughing, and she joined in the conversation by pontificating on some nuggets of handbag wisdom, "Do you realize that as a handbag, we are the only place a man's hands are not welcome? And we are fortunate not to be everyday bags because a Woman's whole life is in her handbag; it's her companion, so we are lucky to have such a long shelf life compared to an everyday handbag. And any bag that holds together longer than your face is a great investment."

The Leiber spoke up, adding to the last statement. "Well, then we are the best investment of all since if you look around this bed, most of us are vintage collectibles."

This speech made all the tiny purses feel useful, even if for just this one night.

As the evening marched on, a few bags left early with the owners who had small children and had to get home to the sitter, and then there was the middle group who knew when to call it a night. Finally, there were those at the end who picked up their belongings either to head home or go on to a small intimate bar for a nightcap. It was funny how people at parties would leave in these groups, not wanting to draw attention to departing too early, but feeling comfortable when they could follow someone else out the door.

Beady watched as each of her new friends departed, hoping they would run into each other again, knowing the chances were slim. The little Leiber Bear gave her a wink as he was scooped up and it made her smile.

# | SHE |

At some point, the depression set in, for She had nowhere to go that Saturday morning, and since the evening when the Lorna Rae bag had been stolen, the event ran like a bad commercial over and over in her head and would not set her free.

Her thoughts continued to wander, and she wondered whether women have looked at life realistically all these years by wanting to be the Princess; maybe it would be more fun to be the Evil Queen—you would get to do crazy things and cock your head back, throw your mouth open, and let out a wicked laugh that shakes your whole body; it looked like fun. It would beat the heck out of marrying some guy you hardly know and having the pressure of looking nice and being nice ALL THE TIME. In taking it a step further, She went on to conclude that the Evil Queen gets to run a big empire and say what she thinks and she gets to wear black. *You know how we love to wear black*, She thought. *It's slimming and classic. That could be a new slogan: Classic as an Evil Queen.*

It was clear now, and She had reached the point of acceptance that her Lorna Rae bag would not be found and would not be coming home. She had done her best to scan local consignment shops and eBay to see whether the bag was out there and whether the thief would know its significance and try to profit from it since whoever stole it did not get away with many charges to her credit cards, and fortunately, no theft on her identity. She had a flag put on her credit report, and she extended it for another six months just to be safe. She still felt violated that the thief had so much of her personal information, and she refused to think of what had happened to the Lorna Rae.

The next day, She's best friend came by to make sure she was okay, and she brought chocolate croissants for comfort. After they finished the pastry and had a coffee drink, they went to the closet where She was moving items around before her friend arrived. Sometimes when She was stressed, she would either clean the closet, have a fashion show, or just move a few things around only to move them back again.

Her friend sat on the bench as She was rearranging her shoes.

"What do you think happened to the Lorna Rae?" She's friend asked.

It was the question the whole closet wanted to ask and one that She could not even get herself to think, but had to face.

"I don't know," said She. "What does happen to handbags that get stolen? Do they kidnap them as their own or pass them along to someone else? Would they try to sell it?"

"Have you looked for it?" asked her friend.

"Of course. I'm checking eBay every day, and I have a few of my consignment friends on the lookout."

"Or they just threw it away after emptying the contents and trying to steal the credit cards," said She's friend.

"Well, they didn't get away with that. They were only able to use one card and purchased around $2,000 worth of computer equipment."

"I can't bear the thought that someone would just throw such a beautiful bag in the trash. Ugh, that is so wrong."

"Maybe the whore who stole it will take good care of it," said She.

"Are you sure it was a woman?"

"Well, it would have looked odd for a man to leave with it."

"True."

"Who knows? I want to think the bag is fine. The only tip I have is that I think it was a couple who strolled through the busy restaurant and made off with it. I feel so stupid."

"Why?"

"Because I am always so careful, you know, especially when it comes to my handbag."

"Yeah, but you can't prevent these situations all the time."

"I know. What's done is done, along with my potential new romance."

"Are you ever going to talk about what happened?"

"What's there to talk about? He has a girlfriend. And I can't display the fatal female flaw in thinking he will leave her and choose me."

"What do you mean?"

"As women, we are constantly thinking that we can make the man we love fall in love with us, or we can change him into the man we want him to be, and then when we don't, there is this huge disappointment, and for some reason, we are surprised. I don't want to be one of those women, not at my age. In our early dating years, we think that, but now, please."

"Yeah, but what I don't understand is why he invited you out in the first place."

"Who knows? I can't believe I let someone break my heart again. Let's not talk about it anymore."

"Okay, but honey, I'm so sorry. You have been through so much and this, well, this just sucks."

"Thanks, but life goes on, and maybe someday I will meet the right guy."

There was a pause in the conversation and her friend changed the subject.

"Your closet is so cool."

"Thank you; I like it."

She smiled and remembered when she'd had the closet custom-designed a few years ago to include the drawers, wardrobe, and shelves to hold all her investments. It was like that Carrie Bradshaw *Sex in the City* saying, "I like my money right where I can see it…in my closet." She wore her fortune on her back. Not completely true, but she wondered whether it was time to sell off a few more pieces.

She reached up to put a few items away when she noticed the Lorna Rae dust cover on the shelf. She pulled it down and opened the drawstring pouch all the way, as if expecting Lorna Rae to appear like a magician pulling a rabbit out of a hat, but all she found was the tissue paper she had used to stuff the bag to hold its shape, and the additional leather strap remained.

"What is that?" her friend asked.

"It's the dust cover from the Lorna Rae."

"Oh, what's that inside?"

"It's the long leather strap that could be attached so it converted to a shoulder bag. I didn't use it very much, but it did come in handy once in awhile."

"What are you going to do with it?"

"I don't know. Hang onto it for now. Maybe I will have another one someday, although I can't afford one right now."

She gently drew the drawstring closed, folded it in half, and placed it back on the shelf with the rest of the handbags.

## | CLOSET |

After She and her friend left to get another cup of coffee, the handbags looked at each other and could not even speak after what they had heard. Lorna Rae was gone, and they had not been very nice to her at times, and now they would never see her again, so they felt terrible. The matriarch of the closet had died.

The YSL was next to the Lorna Rae dust cover and gently leaned against it and sighed. The handbags had been through a lot with She the past two years, and just when they thought things were looking up and they were safe, this tragic event had happened in their little world. It was quiet in the closet for several days.

# Chapter Seven
# G = GRATITUDE

*Luxury is a necessity that begins*
*where necessity ends.*
— Coco Chanel

She was attending a fancy cocktail party and networking event that was hosted by one of the larger firms her new job represented. The party was held at the estate of some computer software mogul. She ran into a former colleague while making her way through the crowd and he congratulated her on her new job.

"Hey, I heard you joined my friend's team, and I think that's great; what a good fit for you."

"Thank you. I love it there and the people are wonderful."

"I would imagine it's a nice change from your last gig."

"What do you mean?"

This comment made her feel nervous because even though she was still sad about her departure, it was always uncomfortable to be approached about things she considered confidential or "off limits." She shifted the Prada handbag from one arm to the other out of nervousness. And then she realized that her comment had invited a response. Crap.

"I won't name names, but I know you were not treated fairly and you were faced with a no win situation over there; I wouldn't have lasted half as long as you did. From what I've heard, the team is not very pleased with your replacement—did you know that?"

She didn't know what to say.

He continued, "And here's an interesting note; three of the HR people over there were either asked to leave or they 'retired.'" And he made air quotes with his fingers.

"No, I didn't know that; that's too bad."

There were mixed feelings running through her blood; a part of her was horrified and wondered whether she should have stayed to fix the mess while the other part felt the sweetness of revenge. There was that Evil Queen side of her coming through, and she needed to hide it before it showed on the outside; she had a terrible poker face.

Fortunately, he didn't notice and patted her on the shoulder with a parting remark. "Anyway, congratulations again, and I'll see you around."

With that, he was gone, and She made her way back to the buffet table to see whether there was any shrimp left.

Did she want to find out more details about what had happened or would this be an opportunity to take the high road? That wasn't necessary because it was like a light went on and her suspicions were confirmed; those who made her life miserable were finally handled.

She remembered the harassing handwritten notes left in her inbox on her desk that had obviously come from someone in the office. HR seemed unable to trace the material, but a few days later, she received an invoice in her mailbox that had similar handwriting, but she was unable to find out from which department it had been misdirected. Then months later, after one of the HR people was dismissed and her replacement emailed her another invoice from the same vendor, she knew where the harassing mail came from. She stared at her computer and felt the rush of anger and more betrayal when she realized that one of the people harassing her was from HR. She felt like she was in a horror movie when you discover the call is coming from within the house. The very group that was supposed to set the standard was behaving badly.

She knew something was amiss during that time, and she would never be able to prove it, but she decided that was the last straw for her. She left her office that day, clinging to her Lorna Rae, and she did not look back.

A lot had transpired since then, and since there is always a reason for what happens in life, she had no regrets and it was time to stop looking back.

With her new job and new outlook, all of a sudden, it didn't matter to her what was left behind or who said what and what their intentions were. Those who had betrayed her were left to deal with the consequences of their poor decisions, and she had the privilege of learning from the situation—to make sure she didn't let it happen to her again, and to become a better manager in the end. For the first time in months, she didn't feel the burden of the past weighing on her; all of a sudden, it was gone. Funny how all it took was the comment of someone she liked and respected to reassure her of her worth. What an interesting lesson to learn in such a short moment; not only would she forgive and move on, but she hoped to have the foresight to help someone else in the future through a difficult time by passing along a compliment of reassurance about the person's abilities.

As She hovered around the buffet table with her tiny cocktail plate, or what she considered her dinner plate, loaded with shrimp, baby quiche, and crudités, she found herself gazing off into the distance after having such deep thoughts. She was so distracted that she hardly noticed her solitude in this social situation and contemplated getting a glass of wine or enjoying more free food. Sometimes, she felt uncomfortable in these social settings without having someone with her. Normally, she dreaded going to an evening event without a date, but at this moment, it didn't bother her.

She was chewing on a shrimp and gripping the small tail between her fingers when she saw a group of women coming her way. They were the country club set here with their husbands, and they were the type of women who played tennis, attended fundraisers, and made shopping their careers. They were dripping in designer outfits and gripping their high-end handbags in their recently manicured hands. For a moment, She felt frumpy around these high class females until they opened their mouths and the cattiness spewed forth. *Yikes!* she thought, and she hung around only for a few minutes to compliment their outfits, and then she made her way back into the crowd to find a friend who was supposed to be there.

Her friend finally showed up, and She noticed her as she made her way through the sea of people.

"Hi, there!"

"Hey, I was looking for you too," said She's friend.

"This is quite the shindig."

"Where's the shrimp?"

"It's at the table over there; come with me; however, I need a drink first."

"Me too."

As they approached the open bar, her friend noticed a colleague from the interior design world waiting in line.

"Hi, how are you?"

"Great. You look lovely."

She had met the designer years earlier when her kitchen was remodeled, and as a result, she was asked to have a photoshoot of her apartment for a kitchen magazine. The whole process was what you would imagine; so much fun! An editor from Chicago came into town to meet and spend the day interviewing her to write an article to accompany the photos of She working in her kitchen. They had lunch in her favorite bistro and took a few photos, and they then moved on to the French bakery to take more photos to highlight her neighborhood. The article was beautifully written and the photos were amazing. What a thrill to spend the day with such talented people.

The photoshoot was filled with so many fun moments that it was one of those days you didn't want to end.

The three of them continued their conversation for a few minutes and caught up on what they were all up to, and then they said their goodbyes. She mingled through the crowd after her friend left to get home to her husband. She did a fair amount of networking and then called it a night.

❧ ❦ ❧

It was the weekend and raining outside. She was trying to motivate herself to run a few errands, but she got distracted by a messy drawer and then moved on to cleaning the closet—dusting all the hangers and shelves and cleaning all her shoes and lining up everything neatly.

As she moved toward the shelf of handbags, she looked at them and thought about how the relationship some women have with their handbags is sacred. *How often are we told not to delve into another person's handbag, like it's a personal sanctuary that can only be accessed by its owner? And most men won't even touch one when asked to retrieve a small item. A look of horror crosses their faces as if they were asked to purchase tampons or asked, "Does this make me look fat?" They look confused and don't know what to say or do, or they head toward the bag without thinking, and when they approach it, they freeze, turn, and look as though the big boulder from an Indiana Jones film is heading for them and they need to run. Or as one friend's husband said, "It's too difficult to find anything in there anyway."*

When the knock sounded on the door, She was surprised since she was not expecting anyone. The delivery person handed her a large shopping bag that held a box.

"Oh, what's this?" She asked in surprise.

"Sign here, please," said the delivery man, and when She had done so, he added, "Thanks. Have a great day," and he was off.

She was so excited to see what was in the box; she removed it from the bag and daintily untied the ribbon, and finally, she saw the box was from Dior. Her heart started to race and felt like it was going to leap from her body. She lifted the lid, and inside at the top was a handwritten note from her older friend with just three little words, "Lady has arrived."

She squealed and removed the tissue. She lifted the dust-covered bag and opened the drawstring to reveal the pink Lady Dior handbag She had noticed the first evening she had visited her friend's infamous closet.

"Oh, so beautiful," She said, hugging the glossy bag, and then she held it up to admire the handiwork and the gorgeous pink patent leather with the decorative Dior lettered fob that hung from the front handle.

> *Lady is a classic Dior bag, designed by John Galliano, made in different leathers and fabrics with the four fobs spelling DIOR hanging from the handle. The exterior pattern is said to be inspired by one of Mr. Dior's chairs and contains a lovely monogrammed fabric interior with a generous zippered pocket. In 1996, Dior sponsored the Cezanne exhibition at the National Galleries of the Grand Palais, attended by the late Diana, Princess of Wales, who was carrying one of the bags. After that, the bag was renamed the Lady Dior as a tribute to Diana.*

She danced into the closet and set the new bag on the bench on top of the dust cover and stood back to admire its beauty. She placed the box on one of her top shelves and was glad she had spent the morning cleaning the closet. Adding the new lovely bag was the perfect finishing touch. She knew the next step was to call her friend to thank her immediately. She reached out and touched the handbag again and smiled, and then she headed out to find her phone to make the thank you call.

Her friend answered the phone.

"Hello."

"Hi," said She. "I just received your amazing gift. This is too much."

"Oh, my dear, it was nothing. You have seen my closet. I want for nothing, and you deserve a new bag after the tragic end to your Lorna Rae bag."

"Still, this was so generous and I thank you."

"My pleasure. Now you can do me a favor and join me for a fashion show this week. I have tickets and would love for you to join me."

"Are you serious? That is fantastic. I would love to."

"Perfect."

## | CLOSET |

The new handbag was sitting on the bench and appeared to be amused while she looked up and noticed the rest of the bags in the closet staring down at her. There were a few moments of silence while everyone waited for the gorgeous new regal bag to speak. They understood they were looking at a beautiful classic handbag that would now be the queen of the closet, and they were okay with that.

"Hello," the Lady Dior said.

"Hello," the rest of the bags responded in unison like they were taking roll call in grade school.

Their hesitation was brought on because they knew this new bag's place in the closet, and they didn't want to make the same mistakes they had made with the previous Lorna Rae.

"Welcome," said the Balenciaga.

"Thank you. Where am I?" the new bag asked.

The rest of the bags smiled and the Chanel tote responded, "You are a lucky handbag and have entered one of the best closets around. Prepare to have some fun!"

The rest of the bags joined in and made introductions. They chatted for hours about their own stories and filled in the new member on her new owner.

## | SHE |

"New beginnings and having a positive outlook" was She's current motto. She had a new job and was looking forward to attending the Spring Fashion Show with her older friend. She selected an outfit from her closet and was excited to carry the new Lady Dior. She wore her Oscar de la Renta embellished silk top, Lanvin polka dot skirt, and floral Rene Caovilla sling back pumps. She posed on the red carpet by the sponsor backdrop and was thrilled later to see her photo made it to the website and the fashion page.

A few weeks later, She met her older friend for lunch, and then they proceeded to go shopping for the day along a small street in a neighborhood full of small elegant clothing boutiques, art galleries, antique stores, and restaurants. After lunch, they wandered into a vintage jewelry store where She purchased a rhinestone necklace and her friend bought a pearl ring.

At the store, She commented on how beautiful and well-made all the older jewelry was compared to what you found in costume jewelry today.

"Well, you know what they say," her older friend stated. "There's a lot of good reading in an old book. And I'm not just talking about things." There was a twinkle in her older friend's eye.

She laughed out loud when She knew what the little innuendo meant. She had to remind herself that her friend had already experienced so much in life, and even in her twilight, she could still remember what it was like to be young and in love and to have those wonderful sexy experiences.

They spent the rest of the afternoon wandering and ended their day by stopping at a small café to have a little

C&C. It was there they realized how far She had come over the past year from their first meeting at the little French bakery and how her life had gone through a wonderful transformation.

"This is fun," She said. "It reminds me of the first day we met. I am so grateful you took the time to talk to me and came into my life. It would not be the same without you."

"Oh, that's dear," her friend responded. "I feel the same way." They spent the next hour regaling themselves by remembering their fun times spent together over the past year, and they knew there would be more to come.

As they said their goodbyes, She leaned in and gave her friend a warm embrace and they promised to call each other by the end of the week to make arrangements for dinner.

The day felt lighter. She paused on the sidewalk as she headed for home, and suddenly, the breeze released the cherry blossoms; they danced in the air and brushed across her check and landed in her hair. It felt glorious; how wonderful that such a small gesture of nature could make her feel so alive. She spread out her arms, bent back her head, and closed her eyes to embrace the shower of soft pink petals. Out of nowhere, a wave of joy spread through her. She smiled—even the air smelled pink. As she lowered her hands, the new Lady Dior slid from her arm and she softly grasped her in her hand; they smiled.

⁓⁓⁓

Across town, the stolen Lorna Rae cowered on a shelf in her captor's closet. It had been weeks since her incarceration, and the time in solitary confinement was taking its toll. There were no other handbags around, and she had spent most of the time lying next to a pile of T-shirts and skinny jeans.

In the evenings, her kidnapper would drink and argue with her boyfriend in a foreign language. The abusive relationship they shared and the environment the handbag was exposed to was a complete contrast to her former life with She. *How can people live this way?* Lorna Rae thought.

The sadness that consumed her was now turning into survival and Lorna Rae knew she had to devise a plan to escape. The handbag began to observe her kidnapper's every move to figure out a way to get transported from the closet and by some miracle back to She....

Made in the USA
Coppell, TX
01 May 2020

23159871R00105